THE HIDDEN WORKSHOP

The Hidden Workshop

ISBN: 979-8-9893424-5-7 (hardback)
979-8-9893424-4-0 (paperback)

Printed in the United States of America

A Christmas Novella

GARY J. ROSE

"In the whimsical realm of Santa's Workshop, nestled amidst the enchanting landscapes of the North Pole, Santa Claus and his diligent elves bring to life the magic of Christmas. Here, in this mystical abode, toys and presents are meticulously crafted with love and care, destined to bring joy to the hearts of children around the world.

While the exact location of Santa's Workshop may vary in local lore, the prevailing belief holds that it exists somewhere in the vicinity of the North Pole. But does Santa and his elves do all the work? Join us as we embark on a journey beyond the ordinary, exploring the wonders of a workshop where dreams are shaped, and the spirit of Christmas comes alive."

The Hidden Workshop

Introduction

"Morning, Frank!" Sarah greeted with a smile wearing her pink scrubs and hair in a ponytail. She gestured for him to join her in the examination room. "How are you doing today?"

"So far, so good, but let's see how I feel after the doc fills me in on those x-rays," he replied.

"Since this is just a consult, we won't need to check your weight or blood pressure. Take a seat here, and I'll go find Dr. Caldwell." With that, she left the room, leaving the door partially closed behind her.

With his coughs escalating in intensity, Frank couldn't shake the growing unease that lingered in the air. Each raspy exhale seemed to echo the anxiety building within him. As he sat on the examination table, the sterile room closed in around him.

As minutes ticked away, Frank's mind began to wander to the possibilities that awaited him. The echo of his coughs served as a disconcerting reminder of the uncertainty that lay ahead. A myriad of thoughts raced through his mind, fueled by the ominous cadence of his own breath. The sterile walls seemed to absorb his apprehension, casting shadows that danced with the flickering fluorescent lights above.

Despite Sarah's earlier attempt to lighten the mood, Frank couldn't escape the nagging feeling that something more profound was at play. The familiar routine of a medical consultation had taken a somber turn, and the impending revelation from Dr. Caldwell hung in the air like an unspoken truth.

As the door creaked open, revealing Dr. Caldwell's arrival, Frank braced himself for the moment of reckoning. The doctor's expression, usually composed and reassuring, now betrayed a subtle gravity. Without a word, Dr. Caldwell pulled up the x-ray images on the screen, and Frank's heart sank. The images painted a stark picture, one that mirrored the increasing severity of his coughs.

The room fell silent as the doctor carefully chose his words, navigating the delicate balance between honesty and compassion. The weight of the diagnosis settled in, and Frank found himself grappling with the reality that unfolded before him. The once-ambiguous worry now crystallized into a tangible concern, casting a shadow over the otherwise ordinary consultation room.

In that moment, as the implications of his worsening condition sank in, Frank's thoughts turned to the journey that lay ahead. The sterile room, once a backdrop to routine check-ups, now bore witness to a pivotal moment that would reshape his life. As he faced the unknown, Frank drew a deep breath, not to stave off another cough, but to muster the strength needed for the challenging road that awaited him.

Christmas Eve

The journey to Uncle Frank and Aunt Susie's log cabin unfolded like a picturesque tale, painting the perfect backdrop for Nancy's 9th Christmas. The road meandered through a winter wonderland, adorned with snow-laden fir trees that whispered tales of the season. Nancy, eager to share the enchanting scene with her seven-year-old brother, Danny, was disappointed to find him sound asleep, oblivious to the beauty surrounding them.

Nancy's father, a festive soul who transformed into a holiday-spirited Clark Griswald, serenaded the family with the familiar tune, 'Over the river, and through the woods, to Uncle Frank's we go.' The melody rang through the frosty air, met with the delighted laughter of her mother. The song served as a beacon, signaling their imminent arrival at the cabin in the woods, a place steeped in cherished Christmas memories.

As they approached, Nancy marveled at the familiar two-story log cabin, seemingly more expansive than in previous years. Perhaps, she mused, it was because, in the past nine years, her focus had been on reaching their destination and preparing for the much-anticipated visit from Santa.

The log cabin, a testament to Uncle Frank's craftsmanship, had a storied history. Built under his watchful eye after retirement, Uncle Frank and Aunt Susie initially resided in a cozy camper on the property. The construction of a garage provided them with a more spacious dwelling, making their accommodations comfortable while the main cabin took shape.

Eagerly racing ahead of her parents and her brother, Nancy was greeted at the front door by Aunt Susie. "My, you've gotten so big. Let me look at you," Aunt Susie exclaimed. Nancy awaited the familiar annual kiss on the forehead and a warm embrace before being released into the grand room of the cabin, where a colossal, freshly cut Christmas tree stood, patiently awaiting her delighted gaze. Danny executed a move around his Aunt Susie, avoiding her kisses and hugs.

"He's at that age," Nancy's mom said. "He won't even let me hug and kiss him in front of people."

"Oh well, that's alright. He will come around when he wants some cookies," Aunt Susie replied, hiding any hurt feelings.

The ambiance within was reminiscent of a scene from a Norman Rockwell painting or a Hallmark Channel special. The crackling warmth from the rock-faced fireplace cast a cozy glow, amplifying the festive cheer that permeated the air. God had bestowed a white Christmas upon them, as gentle snowflakes continued to dance from the heavens, adding an ethereal touch to the holiday setting.

As Nancy's father brought in their luggage and her mother attended to her brother, the scene unfolded like a cherished Christmas card, each element contributing to the magic of this special holiday retreat.

"Ho ho ho!" echoed through the cabin as Nancy's dad, laden with luggage, made his triumphant entrance. Emerging from the kitchen, Uncle Frank wore a broad grin on his face, curious about the source of the festive commotion.

"What's all the yelling about?" he playfully inquired, greeting Nancy's mom with a kiss on the cheek and enveloping her dad in a warm hug. Both her dad and Uncle Frank had enlisted in the U.S. Navy shortly after the bombing of Pearl Harbor. Nancy's dad, a year older than Uncle Frank, came from a large family. Besides them were a sister named Isabel, Uncle Manley, and the youngest of the clan, Uncle Joe, who happened to be Nancy's godfather.

Uncle Frank and Nancy's dad had initially been assigned to different ships due to something called the Sullivan Brothers incident. As Nancy understood it, the tragic event involved five Sullivan brothers of Irish American descent serving together on the USS Juneau during World War II, and they all perished in and around its sinking in November 1942.

In the aftermath, a decision was made to prevent such devastating losses to a single family. Henceforth, no two brothers would serve in the same situation or on the same ship. Or something along those lines. Despite this precaution, during the war, Nancy's dad and Uncle Frank found themselves on the same ship for a brief period after both underwent medical procedures. Fate smiled upon them, granting the luxury of having beds right next to each other during those challenging days.

Childless but overflowing with love, Uncle Frank and Aunt Susie consistently crafted delightful activities for Nancy to revel in while eagerly awaiting the arrival of Christmas Day. The era of dolls had passed for Nancy, and with baby Danny peacefully slumbering, the playthings laid out were solely for Nancy's amusement. Without hesitation, she plunged into word search magazines and an array of toys spread before her.

"Hey everyone, there's all kinds of cookies and pastries in the kitchen, so help yourselves. That includes you too, Nancy. Oh, and there's some hot chocolate on the stove waiting for you," Aunt Susie announced. Nancy left her book on the floor beside the fireplace and Christmas tree, rushing to the kitchen where Aunt Susie was in the midst of pouring her a cup. "Help yourself to the cookies. I made those chocolate chips especially for you."

Balancing her cocoa with care, Nancy treaded back to the grand room, ready to immerse herself in the joyous solitude of play. Meanwhile, her parents joined Uncle Frank and Aunt Susie in a spirited marble game at the kitchen table, swapping stories and catching up on the nuances of life since their last reunion.

Uncle Frank, a perpetually smoking presence, seemed to have a cigarette in an ashtray even as he lit another one. Nancy, mindful of her sensitivity to the smoke, consciously kept her distance during his smoking sessions, taking refuge from the puffs that made her cough. Despite this, the room buzzed with the warmth of family, the crackling fireplace, and the anticipation of the festive season.

The inhabitants of the house were stirred awake on Christmas Day, courtesy of Nancy's strategic cacophony, rousing each member from their slumber. The bountiful array of gifts under the Christmas tree obscured the lower branches, evidence of Santa's industrious visitation. Eager to dive into the festivities, Nancy began the hunt for her presents, only to be intercepted by her vigilant mom, who reminded her to exercise patience.

Aunt Susie, exhibiting a swifter morning rise than Uncle Frank, promptly embarked on the creation of what everyone affectionately referred to as her grand Christmas brunch. A lavish spread unfolded: scrambled eggs, pancakes, sausage, and hash brown potatoes, a culinary spectacle that transformed breakfast into a feast.

Nancy soon discovered that, regardless of how swiftly she devoured her meal, she'd still have to bide her time until the adults completed their repast before delving into the treasures Santa had left for her. The recollections of Nancy's early Christmases would linger eternally in her memory.

2

Fifteen Years Later

"In the university's dining hall, Tim asked Nancy, 'What time are you leaving for your uncle's cabin?' The two had been a couple for the entire last semester. Both seniors, they were set to graduate the following May. Tim's path led to the University of California, Davis, where he would pursue his doctorate in veterinary medicine. In contrast, Nancy would enter the University of San Francisco School of Law.

"I'll be leaving when the sun comes up. It will take me about four hours and I want to get a jump on a snow storm my mom told me is heading that way."

At the age of twenty-four, Nancy blossomed into a stunning young woman, commanding attention with her statuesque 5'7" frame whenever she graced a room. Her long dark brown hair complimented her very dark eyes, almost black as a raven.

Beyond her physical allure, Nancy's accomplishments spoke volumes about her character. A recipient of a full scholarship for her prowess in volleyball, she seamlessly balanced her athletic achievements with a stellar straight-A academic record, securing her place in any law school she desired.

The significance of Nancy's scholarship wasn't lost on her retired parents, who found solace in the fact that their daughter's educational dreams were within reach. Financial constraints would have otherwise made such aspirations unattainable, and they were grateful for the opportunities afforded by Nancy's athletic talents.

However, Nancy's family narrative took a divergent turn when it came to her brother, Danny. Troublesome from his high school days, Danny's life seemed entangled with a series of misadventures, often leading him into clashes with the law. His journey took a dark turn with a year-long stint in the county jail, marking a grim chapter in the family's history.

In stark contrast to Nancy's commitment to education and sports, Danny's aspirations took a more dubious route. Eschewing the pursuit of a stable career or trade, he was perpetually drawn to the allure of quick, albeit illicit, monetary gains. Danny seemed to be content honing his questionable skills, navigating a treacherous path in search of fast money, leaving the family torn between pride for one child and concern for the other.

Aware that their academic pursuits would diverge, even though they'd still be in the same state, Tim and Nancy recognized the strain it might put on their relationship. This Christmas season, they chose not to dwell on the impending separation. While they had spent Thanksgiving together near the campus, the looming holiday would see them heading in different directions. Tim planned to return home to Texas, while Nancy would embark on her trip to Uncle Frank's cabin, where she would reunite with her parents, brother, his girlfriend, and Uncle Frank.

Exactly ten years ago, on November 1st, Aunt Susie had succumbed to cancer. Her passing had deeply affected Uncle Frank, yet he insisted on joining Nancy's parents to celebrate what he affectionately called 'turkey day.' Nancy couldn't help but smile, recalling his words from almost every Thanksgiving: 'Thanksgiving is an easier holiday to celebrate,' he used to say. 'You don't have to worry about buying the perfect gift. Nope, all you had to worry about were the three Fs: Family, food, and football.'" Uncle Frank was Nancy's favorite uncle.

The cherished tradition of the annual Christmas gathering at the cabin came to an unexpected halt after the heart-wrenching loss of Aunt Susie, whose battle with an aggressive form of cancer left an indelible mark on the family. In the wake of her passing, Uncle Frank, usually a prominent presence at these festive reunions, became a shadow of his former self.

His appearances were limited to the Christmas dinner hosted at Nancy's parents' house, where he'd politely participate in the festivities but promptly depart after the presents were unwrapped. Mysteriously, he'd always cite a barrage of tasks awaiting him at home when pressed for an explanation by Nancy's concerned father.

However, this particular year held a promise of change when Uncle Frank made an unexpected call to Nancy's parents. There was a palpable eagerness in his voice as he expressed his desire to revive the cherished tradition of hosting the Christmas gathering at the cabin, just like fifteen years gone by. The caveat: Uncle Frank requested that Nancy's mom take charge of the dinner preparations.

Intrigued and cautiously optimistic about the prospect of reclaiming the familial joy that once radiated from the cabin during the holidays, Nancy's parents agreed to Uncle Frank's proposal. The air was thick with a mix of excitement and curiosity as the family prepared for the upcoming gathering, their minds brimming with questions about the sudden change of heart in Uncle Frank.

As the day of the gathering approached, whispers of anticipation filled the air. Nancy's family wondered if this year's Christmas at the cabin was a return to the warmth and togetherness of years past, or if Uncle Frank's mysterious demeanor would persist. Nancy's mom, taking charge of the dinner preparations with a blend of nostalgia and hope, couldn't help but wonder what had prompted Uncle Frank to break away from his self-imposed solitude.

Nancy's mother found herself preoccupied with worries about the possible encounter between Uncle Frank and Danny's girlfriend, Ginger, as he was known for being forthright and speaking his mind. The fact that he was elderly only heightened her concerns. Referring to Ginger as a "free spirit" might have been an understatement, and there was a sense of uncertainty about whether Danny would indeed undergo positive changes after his time in incarceration, especially considering his choice of a romantic partner.

The prospect of them spending a couple of days together in Uncle Frank's cabin added an extra layer of uncertainty to the situation, leaving Nancy's mother with a sense of both curiosity and apprehension about the unfolding dynamics.

She had snow chains if she needed them, since her mom told her that there was a very good chance of a white Christmas. In her shiny blue 1956 Chevy, she had nestled beside her on the front seat, a hot Cinnabon and a thermos of steaming coffee awaited her. Before embarking on the four-hour drive, she shared a Christmas present and a lingering embrace with Tim.

She found a radio station that was playing non-stop Christmas songs and found herself singing 'Over the river and through the woods..." with a smile on her face. Halfway to her destination, she pulled into a rest area and used the facilities before returning to her warm car to eat her pastry and a cup of coffee. She hoped that her mom and dad liked the gifts she had picked out for them as well as Uncle Frank. Each year it seemed to be harder and harder to select a gift for him.

Nancy's mom had shared with her that ever since the passing of Aunt Susie, Uncle Frank had gradually transformed into more of a homebody – a recluse. This shift in his lifestyle was noteworthy, considering that, if not for Nancy's parents, it was doubtful that Uncle Frank and Aunt Susie would have embarked on a cross-country trip from California to the East Coast before she was diagnosed with cancer.

In fact, the most memorable aspects of their journey were the unexpected encounters with iconic figures like Roy Rogers and Dale Evans at a tourist stop and their visit to the University of Notre Dame.

Uncle Frank's newfound inclination toward home life for the past ten years marked a departure from their earlier, more adventurous escapades. The trip, which might have seemed unlikely in the past, had unfolded as a series of charming encounters and unexpected delights. Meeting Roy Rogers and Dale Evans, legendary figures of the Old West, became an unexpected highlight at a tourist stop. The warmth and authenticity of the encounter left an indelible impression on Uncle Frank and Aunt Susie.

However, the visit to the University of Notre Dame added a touch of history and academia to their journey. The renowned institution, with its storied traditions and architectural grandeur, became a memorable stop that appealed to their curiosity and appreciation for education.

In reflection, Nancy found herself marveling at how these unplanned moments, the chance meetings and educational excursions, had become the heartwarming highlights of her aunt and uncle's once-in-a-lifetime journey. Of course, until her death, Uncle Frank did enjoy an occasional fishing trip.

Presently, as relayed by her mother, Uncle Frank seldom ventures beyond the realms of grocery shopping or doctor's appointments. His activities are now concentrated within his secluded garage, a space that he and Aunt Susie once shared while the main cabin was under construction. Despite its separate identity, the three-car garage, positioned at a considerable distance from the cabin, mimics the size and structure of the main residence. Strikingly off-limits, no one is granted entry into this garage, preserving its mystique and prompting curiosity about its purpose and contents.

In a financial bind, Danny and Ginger found themselves relying on borrowed gas money from friends just to embark on the journey to the cabin. Their trusty, albeit aging, vehicle raised concerns about whether it would withstand the trip. Despite the uncertainties, Danny had already crafted a scheme in his mind.

His plan involved subtly working on Uncle Frank, aiming to extract some much-needed cash from him, all while keeping this covert operation concealed from the watchful eyes of his parents and unsuspecting sister, Nancy. The impending excursion became not just a getaway to the cabin but also an opportunity for Danny to finesse his way into securing some additional funds, setting the stage for a delicate dance of manipulation and financial maneuvering.

Meanwhile, Ginger persistently probed Danny, inquiring about the existence of any valuable items within the house that they could potentially pilfer and later sell upon their return. The duo formed a rather dubious partnership, seemingly fated for additional encounters with the law as their questionable intentions hinted at a penchant for trouble.

Nancy maintained an efficient pace, intermittently updating her parents on the journey's advancement. The absence of snow alleviated the necessity for activating the four-wheel drive. During her travels, she made a brief detour at a fast-food establishment, utilizing the facilities and procuring a burger and soda. Uncertain about the specifics of the Christmas Eve dinner plan, she reasoned that the additional food might prove beneficial, ensuring she was adequately prepared for whatever festivities awaited.

She reached the cabin roughly an hour ahead of Danny and his girlfriend. Welcoming her on the porch, her parents orchestrated a seamless exchange, with her dad taking charge of her luggage. Upon stepping inside, it felt as though a decade had effortlessly dissolved.

The familiar surroundings harkened back to her childhood, preserving the essence of the cabin in a timeless embrace. A roaring fire illuminated the rock-faced fireplace, casting a warm glow across the room, while a freshly cut tree occupied its customary spot, evoking memories of countless Christmas celebrations.

Whether the meticulous preparations were orchestrated by her mom alone or if Uncle Frank had undergone a transformative revelation, akin to Ebenezer Scrooge rediscovering the spirit of Christmas, remained a delightful mystery.

"There she is!" Uncle Frank's familiar voice resonated from the kitchen, a nostalgic echo reminiscent of countless past Christmases. Emerging, he enveloped her in a lingering, heartfelt hug, evoking a flood of cherished memories. As usual, he reeked of cigarette smoke, but that was her Uncle Frank.

The scene seemed almost complete, a tableau of yesteryears, with the only missing piece being Aunt Susie stepping out from the kitchen, bearing a steaming cup of hot cocoa and freshly baked chocolate chip cookies.

"How's my future attorney? How was your trip? You didn't forget how to get here, did you?" he playfully inquired, the warmth of the reunion coupled with a touch of humor, infusing the atmosphere with a sense of familial comfort.

Nancy playfully answered all of Uncle Frank's questions and everyone merged into the kitchen where her mother had prepared for her a cup of chocolate and cookies. "Aunt Susie would be proud mom," Nancy said. Everyone smiles reminiscing about Aunt Susie.

Soon Uncle Frank and Nancy's dad started to watch football in the grand room by the fireplace and Christmas tree while Nancy sat with her mom in the kitchen. "Do you need me to do anything?" Nancy asked. Her mom reassured her that everything was set. A turkey and ham were in the oven just staying warm as were all the side dishes. All that was needed was the arrival of Danny and his girlfriend.

Her mother's voice lingered, a momentary pause suggesting a mind lost in contemplation. "I sure hope everything works out with your brother and Ginger being here," she finally expressed, her tone carrying a mix of concern and reservation. "I shouldn't say this, but I don't really care for her. She's too overbearing and, at times, a know-it-all."

Nancy, absorbing her mother's sentiments, responded empathetically. "You know, I've only met her twice, and I agree. She's not the easiest person to warm up to. I had hoped that after Danny spent time in jail, he would have found someone more, well, appealing and a better role model," she added, a hint of disappointment woven into her words.

The expectation for positive change clashed with the reality of Danny's choice in a partner, leaving an underlying concern about the path he seemed to be continuing down despite the setbacks he'd faced.

A sigh escaped Nancy's mother as she continued, her concern etched across her face. "Your father can't stand her, and I genuinely hope he doesn't get into an argument. You know how your dad is," she confessed, a touch of anxiety creeping into her voice.

"I also wonder how she is going to react with you uncle. He can be so direct. Hope she realizes his age and takes whatever he says with a grain of salt. I'm just hoping for a peaceful Christmas Eve and Christmas Day this year, without any arguments breaking out."

The anticipation of potential discord hung in the air, and Nancy couldn't help but share her mother's wish for a serene holiday gathering. The specter of tension loomed, fueled by her father's evident dislike for Ginger. The desire for a harmonious celebration underscored the importance of familial unity during the festive season, yet the unpredictability of emotions and opinions threatened to disrupt the tranquility they all longed for.

As Nancy began to share with her mom the complexities of her relationship with Tim and the likelihood that their separation due to schooling might lead to the demise of their connection, a sudden backfire from an automobile reverberated across the acreage, causing a startle for both Nancy and her parents. Uncle Frank, unaffected by the auditory disturbance due to his impaired hearing, remained unperturbed.

"That must be Danny," Nancy's mom remarked, exchanging a glance with Nancy, who observed her mother take a deep breath before rising and making her way to the front door. The unexpected interruption added a layer of tension to the already charged atmosphere, leaving an unspoken acknowledgment that the arrival of Nancy's brother might bring a different kind of dynamic to the family gathering.

Nancy's dad gently tapped Uncle Frank who was dozing on his knee, signaling that Danny had arrived. With some assistance, Uncle Frank rose and ambled toward the front door. As Danny parked his car beside Nancy's beautiful Chevy, a parting backfire punctuated their entrance.

Before any conventional greetings could be exchanged, Uncle Frank couldn't help but comment on the car's audible issues. "I think your car needs a major tune-up," he remarked with a wry smile. Nancy loved the fact that elderly people just say whatever comes to their mind without any thought.

Danny, undeterred, quipped, "It needs more than that," while extracting a lone duffle bag from the back seat. Simultaneously, Ginger emerged from the passenger side of the vehicle. Nancy surreptitiously glanced at her mom, who keenly observed Ginger's choice of attire. Despite the near-freezing temperatures and a hint of snowflakes in the air, Ginger sported leather pants that hung low on her hips and a tank top, revealing a black bra underneath.

As Tim followed suit, clad in a wrinkled t-shirt in desperate need of laundering and worn-out jeans with conspicuous holes over the knees, Nancy couldn't decipher if they were deliberately distressed designer jeans or simply well-worn trousers. The stark contrast in attire heightened the family's awareness of the unconventional duo's arrival, raising unspoken questions about their choices and setting the stage for a potentially interesting and unpredictable holiday gathering.

Uncle Frank's hearty greeting resonated on the front porch as he wrapped Danny in a warm hug. "And who the heck is this?" he boomed, a mix of curiosity and amusement in his voice.

"Hey, Uncle Frank. How's it going?" Danny responded, grinning with an air of familiarity.

"It's going. It's going," Uncle Frank replied with a chuckle, diverting his attention to the unfamiliar face beside Danny. "Uncle Frank, this is my girlfriend Ginger."

"Ginger, huh? Just like gingerbread. You need to dress better. You're up here in the mountain's young lady. Can't dress like that. Well, welcome. Come in from the cold and get next to the fireplace to warm up," Uncle Frank genially invited, his jovial tone easing any initial tension. With that, he turned and, as usual, was the first to stride back inside the cabin, leaving a trail of laughter and familial warmth in his wake.

The introduction unfolded, laying the foundation for a potentially intriguing mix of personalities coexisting beneath the same roof, as the family braced themselves to navigate the intricate dynamics of the impending holiday gathering.

Danny, in a seemingly affectionate gesture, planted a kiss on Nancy's cheek, yet the lingering scent of pot wafted in the air. Following suit, Ginger mirrored the gesture, her presence carrying the same distinctive odor.

Once everyone crossed the threshold into the cabin, Nancy's mom assumed her role as the orchestrator of the familial ballet. Uncle Frank retreated to his recliner, engrossed in the football game once again. With authority in her voice, Nancy's mom began issuing directives. She assigned Tim and his girlfriend their designated room within the cabin and informed them that dinner would be served in less than twenty minutes. The bustling activity set the scene for a holiday gathering brimming with diverse personalities and the promise of unforeseen twists in the unfolding narrative.

In the privacy of their bedroom, Ginger turned to Danny, seeking guidance on how to address his Uncle Frank. "Just Uncle Frank. That's what everyone calls him, except maybe his neighbors. Who knows, they might even call him that too. In all the years we used to come up here for Christmas, we never saw any neighbors—just Uncle Frank and Aunt Susie. She passed away nine or ten years ago due to cancer. The old man just lives up here by himself and seems to relish the solitude."

"Damn. Do you realize what this spread of his is worth? How many acres does he have?" Ginger inquired, her eyes widening with a mixture of awe and curiosity.

"I don't know. I never asked," Danny admitted. "I do know he has this large cabin, and way out back, a considerable distance away, there's a garage that's almost equal in size. It's on the other side of the huge pond you saw when we drove up."

"A garage? Don't tell me the old fart still drives. What kind of car does he have in the garage?" Ginger pressed on, her interest piqued. "I've heard that some of these old dudes have cars that would sell for some serious cash at a Barrett - Jackson auction."

"No. He hasn't driven in years. In fact, I remember when I was here one year, that my Aunt did all the driving. They had a four-wheel truck, but after she died, he sold it. He arranges for Uber to pick him up when he has to go to the doctors and normally has the grocery store deliver his food items. Like I told you, after my aunt died, he rarely ventures out."

As they discussed Uncle Frank's property, the allure of the mysterious garage added an intriguing layer to the unfolding narrative. The potential treasures within hinted at the enigmatic life the old man led, sparking Ginger's imagination and leaving them both eager to uncover more secrets of the secluded cabin in the woods.

"Tell me, Danny," Ginger prodded, her eyes fixed on him with a mix of curiosity and suspicion, "why do you harbor so much hate toward your Uncle Frank?"

Danny hesitated, the weight of unresolved resentment hanging heavy in the air. After a moment, he sighed, as if dredging up a painful memory. "I don't really hate him. I guess I'm more disappointed in who he is."

"I used to love coming up here, and not just on Christmas. Sometimes, my dad would drive up here to go fishing with Uncle Frank. That was when he started teaching me to whittle, you know, wood carving."

His gaze drifted off to thoughts of the closed door of the garage, the forbidden space that held the secrets of Uncle Frank's solitude. The mention of whittling brought to mind the intricate details of the hand-carved toys he had admired as a child, now hidden away from prying eyes.

"My uncle is a workaholic. He worked for years driving a bus for Greyhound, until he retired. Then he would come home and hang out for hours in his garage, whittling away. The toys and items he created would then be sold for some pretty good money. The problem was that he didn't need the money. The old man has more money that he knows what to do with. His investments he made in companies I never heard of, gave him outstanding returns, but he never shares it with me."

"My uncle, he's a true artisan, a master whittler, and a skilled wood carver," Danny explained, a touch of pride in his voice. He gestured towards the intricately carved pieces adorning their room in the cabin, evidence of Uncle Frank's once celebrated talent. "Awards used to pour in for his creations, but all of that changed after my aunt passed away. It's like he lost a part of himself with her."

"That still doesn't answer my question," Ginger replied.

"I don't remember how old I was when my uncle first started teaching me the art of whittling wood. My memory is hazy, but the scent of fresh wood chips and the joy of witnessing a simple block of wood transform into intricate shapes of animals, people, and various objects are etched in my mind. It was a magical experience, each carving telling a story of its own."

Danny leaned back in a worn armchair. God, I remember about those early days I spent in the garage with my uncle. The flickering light of the workshop lanterns played against the walls, casting a warm glow on the tools and half-finished creations that adorned the space. The hum of whittling knives against wood became a comforting melody, marking the passage of time. He constantly corrected me if I was doing something wrong, but always praised me at the end of a session."

"One day, my uncle shared a tale about Michelangelo, the multifaceted Italian artist. He described how Michelangelo would study a block of marble, contemplating for hours, envisioning the hidden forms within, urging him to liberate them with his chisel and skill. My uncle adopted a similar approach with wood, regardless of its size. Each block held a world of potential, and he encouraged me to see it the same way."

With a nostalgic smile, he continued, "I honed my whittling skills under his patient guidance, improving with each passing day. Then came the moment when Nancy and I stumbled upon him creating a masterpiece in the garage—a breathtaking merry-go-round. Every carousel horse and animal were a testament to his craftsmanship. Wooden dowels supported the intricately carved top, and a battery-powered motor brought the entire piece to life, turning it with a mesmerizing grace."

His eyes lit up at the memory, reliving the awe of that moment. "I asked him if he could gift it to me for Christmas. Not to be outdone, Nancy chimed in, expressing her interest in some of the other handcrafted toys he had made. But my uncle, ever the wise and fair man, shook his head and said, 'These toys are for sale. If you both want something similar, you'll need to write letters to Santa Claus.' And so, we did."

Danny chuckled at the recollection, the image of his younger self and Nancy earnestly composing letters to the mythical figure. The garage, once a realm of creativity and mentorship, had become a treasure trove of cherished memories.

Ginger chuckled, "So, you're a master carver now, too?"

Danny grinned wryly, "I got pretty good at it, but nowhere near the level of my uncle. He was a true maestro, and carving became a cherished part of our family tradition, especially during the holidays."

Ginger leaned in, her curiosity unabated. "So, spill it. What happened that made you and your uncle drift apart?"

Danny drew in a deep breath, casting a brief glance at Ginger before launching into his tale. "You know, that Christmas when I asked Santa for the merry-go-round, I could hardly contain my excitement. I couldn't wait to dash downstairs and find it nestled under the tree. But, as tradition dictated in our family, we had to endure my aunt's Christmas buffet first." He chuckled before resuming his narrative.

"Eventually, we all gathered in the grand room. Nancy, being the older one, took on the role of Santa Claus, distributing presents one by one – always in a particular order to satisfy my sister's sense of orderliness. I spotted a box that seemed to match the size and shape of the merry-go-round I had wished for, and after what felt like an eternity, my sister handed it to me. Lo and behold, the tag revealed it was from Uncle Frank."

As Danny continued, the laughter in his voice faded, replaced by a tinge of irritation. "Upon tearing open the wrapping, I discovered a sizable plastic bag, its weight betraying the promise of something substantial. I didn't think much of it; after all, some woods are naturally heavy. I untied the string and peered inside, only to find another bag. Laughter erupted around me. Undeterred, I fished out that bag, discovering it was filled with wood blanks – the raw materials for whittling. At the bottom I found a bag that contained coal."

"What?" Ginger asked.

Danny's frustration lingered, a simmering undercurrent that colored his reply, "A bag of coal. A fricken bag of coal. It wasn't exactly a laughing matter at the time." The words carried the weight of a Christmas past, an episode etched in memory despite the years that had passed. The unexpected twist of humor had transformed into a bittersweet recollection, leaving Danny with a lingering sense of disappointment.

Ginger, sensing there was more to the story, leaned in and asked, "So, what did you do?"

A wry smile crossed Danny's face as he recalled the events that followed. "Well, my anger management didn't kick in. I got so upset with everyone laughing that I impulsively hurled the bag of coal at my unsuspecting uncle. The trajectory, fortunately or unfortunately, missed him by a few feet. As the coal sailed through the air, I stood up, my face flushed with a mix of embarrassment and rage, and declared that I hated him."

The room, once filled with laughter, fell into an awkward silence as Danny's outburst took everyone by surprise. His parents, attempting to regain control of the situation, urged him to calm down. However, fueled by a mixture of adolescent rebellion and wounded pride, Danny turned on them too.

"I then turned to my mom and dad," he continued, "and told them that I hated Christmas and, for good measure, that I hated them as well. The atmosphere grew tense as I stormed out of the room, leaving behind a bewildered family and shattered Christmas cheer."

As he recounted the tale, Danny couldn't help but acknowledge the absurdity of his reaction. What had started as a simple, albeit disappointing, Christmas gift had escalated into a moment of rebellion, leaving an indelible mark on his family's holiday memories.

"Wow!" was all that Ginger could say, her eyes wide with a mixture of disbelief and amusement. Danny chuckled at her reaction, acknowledging the absurdity of his own past actions.

"Yeah, it was quite the scene," he admitted, a sheepish grin spreading across his face. "Looking back, I can't believe I let a bag of coal push me over the edge like that. Teenagers, right?"

Ginger nodded, still processing the unexpected turn of events in Danny's Christmas tale. "So, did things get better after that?" she asked, curiosity evident in her voice.

Danny's grin faded, replaced by a more thoughtful expression. "Well, that Christmas was definitely a low point. I wouldn't even come down for Christmas dinner. I only left my room when it was time for us to go home. But over the years, we found a way to laugh about it. It became a family joke, a reminder not to take things too seriously. And, you know, I eventually outgrew my Christmas-hating phase. But my uncle never seemed to get over it. He always had the philosophy of 'forgiven, but not forgotten'."

As he spoke, Danny's gaze seemed to drift into the past, revisiting the memories that had shaped his relationship with the holiday season. Ginger couldn't help but be intrigued by the layers of history embedded in his story.

"So, how about you?" Danny asked, breaking the momentary silence. "Any memorable holiday tales from your past?" Ginger remained quiet for a few minutes; her gaze fixed on a distant point as if navigating the corridors of her own memories. Finally, with tears welling up in her eyes, she opened up.

"My mom left my dad and me when I was only six years old," Ginger began, her voice carrying a mixture of vulnerability and resilience. "She became a hippie and traveled with a rock-n-roll band, never checking in on me. Holidays, especially birthdays and Christmases, were not high on my dad's list of things to celebrate."

As she spoke, there was a palpable weight to Ginger's words, a reflection of the emotional journey she had navigated. Danny listened attentively, sensing the depth of her story.

"We never had a Christmas tree after my mom left. She got into drugs and alcohol and thought that buying a tree and bringing it into the house to watch it die, was stupid. I remember one Christmas in particular," Ginger continued, her voice softer now. "I must have been around ten. Dad was working extra shifts, trying to make ends meet, and I spent most of the holiday season on my own. The apartment felt empty, the absence of festive decorations and laughter making it painfully clear that it wasn't a season of joy for us."

Ginger paused, wiping away a stray tear, and then continued, "I didn't have the heart to ask for presents or even mention the word 'Christmas.' It just felt like a reminder of everything we didn't have. So, I spent that Christmas quietly, finding solace in the little moments of warmth I could create for myself."

Danny, sensing the delicate nature of her story, nodded empathetically, inviting her to share as much or as little as she was comfortable with.

"Anyway, this particular Christmas Eve, my dad came home drunk carrying a grocery bag," Ginger continued, her voice carrying the weight of a memory etched in the lines of her story. "You know, one of those plastic bags that Walmart gives you for your groceries and stuff. He walked in while I was watching television and said, 'I guess I'm supposed to say Merry Christmas,' and tossed the bag to me. Inside was a granola bar and Snickers candy bars. So, like you, I developed this disdain for Christmas."

As she recounted the scene, there was a sense of disappointment in Ginger's voice. Danny listened, understanding the complexities of holiday experiences that weren't always filled with joy and laughter.

"But you know," Ginger continued, her gaze steadying as she shifted from the past to the present, "those challenging times taught me resilience and the value of creating your own joy. Now, every Christmas, I make it a point to break into people's houses and unwrap their gifts taking what I want."

Ginger's words resonated with bitterness, as if she had found a way to transform the Christmases of her past into a source of empowerment. "And you know what," she added, a hint of a smile playing on her lips, "I always make sure there's a granola bar and a Snickers in the mix by the time I get home. It's become my way of acknowledging where I've been and appreciating the journey that brought me to where I am now."

Danny couldn't help but feel a profound connection with Ginger, realizing that the holiday season held a diverse tapestry of stories, each contributing to the unique way people navigated and found meaning in this time of year.

"It got worse on the following Christmases. It all started after Aunt Susie passed away," he began, his gaze distant as he recollected the events of that fateful time. "If my memory serves me right, it was the last Christmas we celebrated here at the cabin." Ginger leaned in, her interest piqued, urging him to continue.

"Anyway, when I was growing up and my aunt was still around, my uncle took me under his wing. He continued to teach me the art of carving, passing down the skills he had honed over the years, but we weren't close anymore."

Danny sighed, a tinge of regret evident in his eyes. "It all went south when I started getting into trouble at school. Suspensions turned into expulsions, and before I knew it, I was a regular at juvenile hall. Every time my uncle saw me, it was like disappointment etched across his face, telling me to grow up and get my act together. He even went as far as suggesting I join the military to straighten myself out."

He paused, the weight of those memories heavy on his shoulders. Ginger studied him, sensing there was more to the story.

"During the final Christmas we spent at the cabin, my uncle unveiled a breathtaking masterpiece—a handcrafted pirate ship that left everyone in awe. The sheer dedication he poured into this creation was evident in every meticulous detail. Measuring approximately one foot in length and standing proud at ten inches, this ship was a testament to my uncle's skill and passion."

"The ship boasted cloth sails, delicately stitched and billowing with imaginary winds, giving it an authentic and dynamic appearance. Perched on a sturdy piece of redwood, it became a captivating centerpiece, commanding attention with its intricate design and artistry. To witness such a work of art was to glimpse the soul of my uncle's craftsmanship, a tangible expression of the hours and love he invested in his carvings." Danny paused as if lost in thought.

"Well, it looks like both of us share a similar perspective on Christmas, but hey, we're here now, and we can play the game," Danny remarked with a wry grin. The twinkle in his eye hinted at a mischievous plan forming in his mind. "Once I think the moment is right, I'll hit up my uncle for some cash."

Ginger couldn't help but smile at Danny's sly determination. "Cash from your Uncle? What's the game plan?"

Danny leaned in, as if about to share a well-kept secret. "Well, my uncle is usually in a good mood during the holidays. I've got this whole strategy worked out. First, I'll butter him up, you know, a few compliments here and there about how he's the 'cool uncle' and all. Then, when he's feeling generous and festive, I'll slip in a subtle request for a little financial boost."

Ginger chuckled, appreciating the blend of humor and chicanery in Danny's approach. "Smooth. So, what's the end game here?"

Danny's eyes sparkled with mischief, and a determined grin played on his lips. "The end goal? To turn this Christmas into one we'll actually enjoy! Whether it's scoring some extra cash or adding a dash of unexpected fun to the festivities, I'm on a mission to rewrite the holiday narrative for both of us. We'll play the game—open presents under the tree tomorrow morning, I'll hit the old man up for some cash, we'll have Christmas dinner, and then get the hell out of here."

As they continued to exchange playful banter, it became increasingly evident that Danny was on a mission to inject a dose of warped cheer into the season, utilizing his unique blend of charm and strategy. His eyes, filled with a mischievous glint, hinted at the unfolding plans in his mind. Ginger couldn't help but feel a mounting sense of anticipation, eagerly awaiting the twists and turns Danny's plot would take and secretly hoping it would indeed alter their Christmas experience for the better.

"Seriously, though," Danny continued, his tone shifting to a more reflective note, "we've had our share of not-so-jolly Christmases. It's time to create some memories that don't involve bags of coal or forgotten presents. We deserve a holiday that's actually worth remembering, don't you think?"

Ginger nodded, appreciating the sincerity beneath Danny's playful exterior. She couldn't deny the appeal of the prospect of rewriting their holiday narrative, and in Danny's determined gaze, she saw a glimmer of hope for a Christmas that transcended the disappointments of the past.

7

Under the crisp, moonlit sky on Christmas Eve, Danny and Ginger, driven by desperation and a misguided sense of entitlement, tiptoed through the snow-laden woods surrounding his uncle's secluded cabin. The warmth of the flickering fireplace and the festive ambiance of the Christmas decorations seemed like distant memories as the couple trudged through the wintry night.

Their breath hung in the air as they reached the imposing silhouette of Uncle Frank's massive garage. The timber structure, wrapped in the mystery of the night, loomed before them like a forbidden fortress. In hushed whispers, Danny and Ginger exchanged nervous glances before attempting to pry open the creaking door. To their dismay, the entrance was secured with an unyielding lock.

As they stood there, contemplating their next move, an eerie hush settled over the hidden workshop. Faint sounds emanated from within, like the distant echoes of hammering and the shuffle of unseen figures. The white-washed windows offered no glimpse into the secrets concealed behind the sturdy walls.

Summoning the courage to proceed, Danny and Ginger exchanged a furtive look before knocking timidly on the door. The quiet night seemed to amplify the hollow thuds, but there was no response. Growing bolder, they circled the workshop, their curiosity overcoming their fear.

Suddenly, a stern voice cut through the silence. "What do you think you're doing?" Startled, Danny and Ginger turned to find Uncle Frank emerging from the shadows. His eyes, glinting with a mix of disappointment and anger, betrayed the gravity of their trespass. He stepped forward, blocking their path to the locked door, and warned them with a voice as cold as the winter air, "No one is allowed in the garage. This is off-limits for a reason. You know this Danny. "

Caught in the act, Danny's ill-conceived plan unraveled before his uncle's disapproving gaze. The hidden workshop, a place shrouded in family lore and holiday enchantment, now stood as a testament to the consequences of selfish intentions on this fateful Christmas Eve.

"I just thought Ginger might appreciate the craftsmanship of your carvings," Danny offered, attempting to downplay the ulterior motive behind their late-night escapade.

A discerning glint sparkled in Uncle Frank's eyes as he regarded his nephew. "Mischief is written all over your face, Danny. The workshop isn't a playground for curiosity seekers. I suggest the two of you head back to the warmth of the cabin before you catch a cold wandering out here," he admonished, his stern expression highlighting both disappointment and concern.

The weight of Uncle Frank's gaze lingered on them, a silent reminder of the familial boundaries they had brazenly trespassed. Ginger, sensing the tension, instinctively clutched Danny's arm. The cold air seemed to cut through their excuses, and with a reluctant nod, they retraced their steps through the snow-covered path back to the cabin.

As they trudged away, the distant glow of the workshop behind them, Danny couldn't shake the feeling of missed opportunity and lingering guilt. Uncle Frank's cautionary words echoed in his mind, emphasizing the significance of the forbidden workshop. It wasn't just a place of creative endeavors; it held the essence of family traditions, secrets, and a legacy that demanded respect.

Little did Danny realize, this fateful encounter would cast a shadow over the remainder of their Christmas Eve, unraveling more than just the ill-fated plan to secure a loan.

Observing their retreat toward the cabin, Uncle Frank embarked on a deliberate stroll around the garage, ensuring its secure state. With each unhurried step, he surveyed the perimeter, checking locks and confirming the sanctity of the hidden workshop.

Casting one final glance at the structure, his gaze held a touch of nostalgia, as if wandering through the corridors of cherished memories from a bygone era.

There, under the pale glow of the moonlight, Uncle Frank took a moment to reflect on the workshop's history — a repository of tales, craftsmanship, and familial bonds. His eyes lingered on the weathered facade, perhaps recalling moments of laughter, shared endeavors, and the echoes of simpler times, including his carving sessions with Danny. With a wistful sigh, he reluctantly tore his gaze away, acknowledging that the past was a treasure chest locked in the recesses of memory.

As Uncle Frank retraced their steps, a sense of solemnity accompanied him, a silent acknowledgment of the secrets concealed within the workshop's sturdy walls. The night enveloped him as he headed back toward the cabin, the weight of untold stories and the echoes of past joy lingering in the winter air.

Christmas morning unfolded, and like clockwork, Nancy was the earliest riser in the household, a tradition that had endured since her childhood. Instead of her former exuberant approach, however, she tiptoed into the kitchen, a realm where the intoxicating aroma of brewing coffee wafted through the air. As the coffee machine hummed to life, she found solace in the stillness of the early hours.

A tempting array of her mom's leftover chocolate chip cookies beckoned from the table, patiently awaiting the perfect pairing with the soon-to-be-ready coffee. Nancy indulged in the sweet treats, savoring the familiar taste that carried the essence of holiday mornings gone by. Just as the anticipation of the day's festivities began to settle, Uncle Frank, clad in an oversized bathrobe, emerged, drawn by the irresistible scent of fresh coffee.

"Gee, you're up bright and early. Old habits die hard, huh? Coffee brewing?" Uncle Frank inquired with a characteristic grin, reaching for his renowned hand-crafted coffee cup.

Nancy, enveloped in the warmth of the moment, nodded with a soft smile. "Yeah. Do you remember all those mornings when I used to get up early and practically announce to the entire house that Santa had paid us a visit?"

A nostalgic glint flickered in Uncle Frank's eyes as he recalled the memories of Nancy's childhood Christmases. "Of course I do. When you and Danny were just a little ones, your aunt and I would sometimes already be awake in our room, waiting to hear the unmistakable sound of you two bounding down the stairs to check on the presents. 'Any minute now,' your aunt used to say, and right on cue, you two would burst forth, yelling at the top of your lungs that Santa had worked his magic during the night. Do you remember when sometimes I acted that I was still asleep and you aunt would tell you two that you needed to wake up Uncle Frank?"

Nancy laughed while nodding in remembrance. The resonance of those treasured moments lingered in the air, interwoven with their shared laughter, creating a bridge between the bygone years and the present on this enchanting Christmas morning. Following the reminiscing, Nancy's mom made her entrance, cocooned in a pristine white bathrobe and complementing slippers.

"Good morning. You two are up bright and early," she greeted, acknowledging the early risers with a warmth that mirrored the comforting ambiance of the holiday season. The gentle hum of the coffee machine signaled the completion of its task, adding a symphony of familiar sounds to the festive atmosphere.

At last, Nancy's dad strolled into the room, already clad in his daywear, a testament to his readiness for the festivities ahead. He greeted the early risers with a raised eyebrow and a lighthearted remark, "Doesn't anybody believe in sleeping in these days?"

His brother, Uncle Frank, never one to pass up an opportunity for banter, retorted with a playful grin, "What, you think you need more beauty sleep?" The exchange of jests sparked a ripple of laughter, adding a touch of camaraderie to the Christmas morning scene. The familial banter echoed the easygoing spirit that characterized their gatherings, a tradition as enduring as the twinkling lights and the scent of pine that enveloped the holiday festivities.

After Uncle Frank poured the initial cup from the coffee machine, a synchronized ritual ensued as everyone else followed suit. Seated around the inviting kitchen table, each member of the family reached for a tempting cookie, the sweet accompaniment to their morning coffee. A subtle air of anticipation enveloped the room, accentuated by Uncle Frank's contemplative demeanor. It was evident to everyone that he harbored something on his mind, a sentiment that lingered unspoken.

As they sipped their coffee and nibbled on cookies, a collective curiosity hung in the air. It became apparent that Uncle Frank was grappling with a desire to articulate something significant, yet the words seemed to elude him. Sensing the unspoken tension, Nancy took it upon herself to shatter the silence that held sway over the cozy kitchen.

"Uncle Frank," she began, her voice cutting through the quietude, "are you ever going to share with us what prompted you, after all these years, to host a white Christmas here at your cabin, reminiscent of the years gone by?"

The question hung in the air, echoing with the unspoken inquiry that had subtly pervaded the room. The family's collective gaze shifted towards Uncle Frank, awaiting the revelation that seemed to linger on the brink of disclosure.

Uncle Frank took a long sip of his coffee and leaned forward. "Actually, I'm glad that the three of you were the first to come down this morning. I need to share something with you." He paused for a long time and then took another sip of his coffee. This can't be good, Nancy thought to herself.

"A few months ago, "I got diagnosed with lung cancer," he admitted, his tone carrying a mix of solemnity and a hint of gallows humor. "If you smoke like a train, you know it's bound to catch up with you sooner or later." Despite the weight of his words, Uncle Frank injected a touch of levity into the conversation, a characteristic attempt to ease the gravity of what he was about to reveal.

"The doc handed me a prognosis—six months, tops. And well, here we are, four months into that countdown," he shared, his eyes reflecting the acceptance of a reality that had unfolded in the shadows. The revelation hung in the air like a heavy cloud, casting a somber hue over the kitchen that had moments ago buzzed with the festive spirit of Christmas morning.

Nancy, absorbing the weight of Uncle Frank's revelation, exchanged a glance with her mom, realizing that tears were now unavoidable. In the face of the unexpected news, emotions spilled forth, and a shared vulnerability embraced the room. Nancy and her mom, overcome by the reality of Uncle Frank's diagnosis, succumbed to tears, the unspoken acknowledgment of the impending farewell that loomed over their holiday gathering.

The usual merriment of Christmas morning now intertwined with a bittersweet undertone, as the family grappled with the delicate balance of joy and sorrow, celebration and farewell.

"I realize it might sound futile to ask you both not to shed tears, but I've been blessed with a good life," Uncle Frank acknowledged, his tone carrying a mix of acceptance and gratitude. "Father Paul over at St. Teresa has already administered the last rites, and I'm at peace, ready to reunite with Susie.

Nancy, I know you're not officially a lawyer yet, but I've appointed your dad as the executor of my will and trust. I'm counting on you to navigate through all the bureaucratic nonsense, so whatever I leave behind finds its way to all of you, not the darn government."

Uncle Frank's words, imbued with a blend of practicality and a touch of humor, aimed to lighten the somber moment. The weight of his impending departure hung in the air, but the shared responsibility and familial bond forged a promise to honor his wishes amidst the looming shadows.

"Now, I need you three to make me a solemn promise," Uncle Frank urged, his gaze shifting between Nancy, her mom, and her dad. The weight of his request carried a gravity that demanded attention. "Promise me that once I'm gone, my workshop, my sacred garage, remains untouched. Let Mother Nature reclaim it. The place has its own deed, so if the day comes when you decide to sell the cabin, that's alright. But the garage – it must stand, a silent witness to the stories it holds. I don't want the land sold until it has gracefully returned to its natural state."

Uncle Frank's plea resonated with a profound sense of attachment to the workshop, a space that transcended mere bricks and mortar. It was a repository of memories, a sanctuary of creativity, and a testament to the legacy he hoped would endure. The request to let the workshop return to nature held the echo of a final wish, a pact to preserve a piece of his world that had been woven into the fabric of the family's history. The room fell into a contemplative silence, the weight of the promise lingering in the air, binding them to a pact that transcended time.

"The trust, which I've recently had an attorney review, should streamline everything and make it easy to follow," Uncle Frank explained, leaning into the assurance of legal arrangements.

Turning his attention to Nancy, he continued, "So, to answer your question, niece, I wanted one last family gathering here at the cabin that holds so many special memories for me." The revelation of his impending departure was met with a somber understanding, as the weight of the occasion settled over the kitchen.

As Uncle Frank shared this poignant moment, he sensed a presence lingering just around the corner of the kitchen entrance. Though his eyes flickered in that direction, he revealed no acknowledgment of the unseen observer.

His intuition proved correct, for outside the door, Ginger stood, her ears absorbing the poignant conversation. With a hurried yet quiet return to the room, she leaned in to share the information with Danny, her eyes betraying a mix of excitement and cunning.

"You're on your way to becoming a millionaire," she whispered to Danny, who was just rousing from his slumber. Blinking away sleep, he questioned, "What are you talking about?" The room buzzed with a blend of anticipation and confusion, as the unfolding events hinted at a turn of fortune that Danny had yet to comprehend.

"Your uncle is dying. He has lung cancer with only a few months left. That means, soon, you will inherit a ton of money."

"What? How do you know that?" a still groggy Danny asked.

"As I was going down the stairs toward the kitchen, intending to grab a cup of coffee and enjoy some of your mom's cookies, I overheard your uncle revealing to those present in the room that he had only a few months left to live.

He mentioned that his will and trust were already arranged, with your dad serving as the executor of the trust. This means that when the time comes, you will inherit a significant amount of money, primarily from this cabin alone, without even considering his other assets."

Danny remained silent, his emotions in tumult. Memories of the good times spent with his uncle in the garage, whittling away together and engaging in heartfelt conversations flooded his thoughts. Guilt washed over him as he reflected on the years of being distant and standoffish, accusing his uncle of being miserly and withholding his wealth.

"Did you hear me?" Ginger asked a little perturbed. "You're going to be rich. I wonder how many exact months he has left? Do you think your dad will sell the cabin and acreage as soon as he dies? I heard him ask them to promise never to sell the garage, but heck, after he is gone, they should sell it also and split the proceeds."

"Well, aren't you the schemer? My uncle isn't even laid to rest, and you're already envisioning the division of his assets. Let me mull this over. I'll get dressed, and we can join them in the kitchen. Let's see who fills us in on his health."

A few minutes later they walked into the kitchen. "How did the two of you sleep?" Nancy's mom asked. "I hope I gave you enough blankets," she added.

Uncle Frank's penetrating gaze lingered on Ginger, a silence hanging in the air that made her squirm with discomfort. Finally, breaking the stillness, he bluntly remarked, "You know, young lady, you might actually be considered beautiful if you didn't insist on adorning yourself in such... well, let's just say, provocative attire." The weight of his words seemed to accentuate the awkward tension in the room, leaving Ginger feeling self-conscious under his critical scrutiny.

Ginger, forewarned by Danny about his uncle's penchant for straightforwardness and lack of political correctness—something he took pride in—responded to Uncle Frank's critique with a wry smile. "Well, thank you for the, uh, compliments, I guess. By the way, do I detect the aroma of fresh coffee?" As she and Danny made their way towards the coffee maker, the lingering tension in the air began to dissipate, replaced by the comforting fragrance of brewing coffee. The brief exchange served as an unexpected icebreaker, diffusing the awkward atmosphere and paving the way for a more relaxed interaction.

The group, with the exception of Uncle Frank, decided to shift their seating arrangement at the kitchen table to make room for Ginger and Danny. Danny's father, leaning against the table, directed his attention to his brother, Uncle Frank. "Frank, would you mind updating Danny on your current situation?"

Uncle Frank, seemingly uninterested, responded, "Nah, you go ahead. I've got some things to sort out in my garage. I'll be back in an hour or two." With those words, Frank rose from his seat, bundled up against the chilly air, and exited the cabin, leaving the others to address the impending conversation with Danny.

"I have some bad news." A heavy atmosphere enveloped the room as Danny's father solemnly began to share the distressing news. "Uncle Frank has recently revealed to us that he's been diagnosed with lung cancer, and the doctors have given him only a few months to live. I understand that the two of you shared a close bond at one point."

The weight of the revelation hung in the air, casting a somber shadow over the room. Nancy and her mother, unable to contain their emotions, were once again overcome with tears. The gravity of Uncle Frank's situation weighed heavily on everyone present, and the room was filled with a profound sense of sadness and empathy for the impending challenges that lay ahead.

Attempting to feign surprise, Danny made a conscious effort to conceal the knowledge that Ginger had already discreetly filled him in on the sensitive information. Despite having overheard the earlier conversation in which he wasn't meant to be a participant, Danny endeavored to maintain a facade of surprise, understanding the delicacy of the situation.

Internally conflicted, Danny found himself grappling with the delicate balance of maintaining appearances while simultaneously carrying the emotional weight of the news that was now being officially disclosed to him. Ginger's advance revelation had injected an additional layer of complexity into Danny's response, forcing him to navigate the challenging terrain of aligning his genuine emotions with the expected surprise in the wake of the freshly shared revelation.

In this intricate dance of emotions and social dynamics, Danny endeavored to uphold the sensitivity of the moment. However, beneath the surface of feigned surprise and genuine concern, a pragmatic thought lingered in the recesses of his mind—the inevitable inheritance that would come his way once his uncle's passing occurred. Despite the heavy emotional toll, the practical aspects of the situation subtly played a role in Danny's internal struggle, adding a nuanced dimension to his response to the impending reality of his uncle's prognosis.

"Do we know exactly how much time he has left?" Danny asked as delicately as he could. He posed the question delicately, concealing the underlying curiosity that lingered in his mind. While he genuinely cared about his uncle's well-being, a more pressing concern was veiled behind his inquiry—specifically, the timeline for the inheritance and when his family would decide to sell the cabin and land following his uncle's passing, ultimately determining when Danny could secure his rightful share.

"Four months or less," Nancy revealed, the weight of the impending loss evident in her voice. "That's why he gathered us here one last time to celebrate Christmas together."

As the somber reality settled over the room, Nancy turned to her brother, Danny, her eyes reflecting a mixture of sadness and concern. "Can I ask you a question, brother?"

Feeling a subtle uneasiness creeping in, Danny attempted to mask it with a façade of bravado. "Of course, Sis. Shoot, what do you want to ask me?" Despite his outward show of confidence, beneath the surface, Danny couldn't escape the underlying tension, aware that the impending question might delve into the intricacies of the family dynamics and the forthcoming inheritance discussions.

As the somber reality settled over the room, Nancy turned to her brother, Danny, her eyes reflecting a mixture of sadness and concern. "Can I ask you a question, brother?"

Feeling a subtle uneasiness creeping in, Danny attempted to mask it with a façade of bravado. "Of course, Sis. Shoot, what do you want to ask me?" Despite his outward show of confidence, beneath the surface, Danny couldn't escape the underlying tension, aware that the impending question might delve into the intricacies of the family dynamics and the forthcoming inheritance discussions.

Nancy's concern lingered in the air as she delicately broached a sensitive topic. "Maybe it's just me," she began, choosing her words with care, "but there still seems to be a lingering sense of animosity between you and Uncle Frank. What caused the split between the two of you? You were both so close."

The question hung in the air, prompting a reflective pause. Danny, momentarily caught off guard, shifted uncomfortably in his seat. The memories of the fracture in his relationship with Uncle Frank resurfaced, and he grappled with the complexities of how things had changed between them over time.

As he began to respond, Danny's bravado waned, revealing a vulnerability beneath the surface. He started recounting the gradual drift that had occurred, the unspoken tensions that grew, and the underlying issues that had strained their once-close bond. The room, now thick with a mix of emotions, became a space for unraveling family history and the intricate dynamics that had led to the apparent estrangement.

Everyone noticed Ginger place her hand under the table apparently to touch Danny's leg for support. As the room held its breath, Danny took a deep sigh, allowing the weight of years of unspoken resentment to surface. "You want to know why there's tension, Sis?" he began, his gaze fixed on a point in the distance as if searching for the right words. "It's because of the money."

The words hung heavy, and Nancy's eyes widened with surprise. "Money?" she questioned, urging him to elaborate.

"Yeah, money," Danny continued, his voice tinged with a mixture of frustration and hurt. "Uncle Frank has this stash of money, and he never shares it with the family. I mean, he's got these incredible handmade whittling items that he sells worldwide, and the money just goes into his bank account. Remember that Christmas where all I asked for was the wooden ship he made, and he gave me a bag of coal?"

He paused, grappling with the flood of emotions that accompanied this revelation. "We grew up with struggles, and now he's got all this wealth, but it never trickles down to us. It's like he's building this fortune, and we're left to fend for ourselves. That's what changed between us. It's not just a personal split; it's a divide caused by a lack of generosity, a sense of abandonment."

The room seemed to hold its breath as Danny laid bare the raw truth, finally expressing the deep-seated hurt that had fueled the perceived animosity between him and Uncle Frank. The complexities of family dynamics and financial disparities were now laid bare, casting a shadow over the otherwise sentimental gathering.

Danny's father, growing perturbed at his son's apparent ingratitude, confronted him with a pointed question. "Who do you think paid for Nancy's undergrad tuition?" he queried, emphasizing the financial support provided. "And who do you think bought you and Nancy your cars? It wasn't us," he added, sharing a pointed glance with his wife.

"Oh, yeah. Nancy, Nancy. Always Nancy. We all know she's his favorite," Danny scoffed, his bitterness evident. "So, he bought me a car, but did he offer assistance when it got into an accident?"

"Danny, you were driving drunk and hit that power pole. Thank God no one got hurt," his mother interjected, a mix of concern and reproach in her tone.

With a scornful tone, Danny retorted, "Oh, yeah. It's my fault." The room crackled with tension as the unspoken grievances between Danny and his uncle bubbled to the surface. The financial assistance provided to Nancy became a point of contention, and Danny's dissatisfaction with his perceived lack of support during challenging times emerged as a focal point in the conversation.

The family dynamics, strained by financial disparities and personal choices, unfolded in a complex tapestry of emotions and discord.

"Enough!" Danny's father thundered, the force of his shout reverberating through the room as his hand came crashing down on the kitchen table. A few chocolate chip cookies jumped out of their plate. The sudden outburst silenced the gathering, casting a momentary stillness over the emotionally charged atmosphere.

"He's dying," Danny's father continued, his voice now measured but firm. "Whatever has happened in the past must be set aside so that he can enjoy one final Christmas with us. I implore you all to put aside grievances and be civil with him for the sake of this holiday."

The weight of his words lingered, emphasizing the urgency to set aside personal differences and prioritize the limited time they had left with Uncle Frank. The plea for civility echoed through the room, a call to find a common ground amidst the discord that threatened to overshadow the spirit of Christmas. It was a heartfelt plea, a reminder that even in the face of unresolved issues, the bonds of family should prevail during this precious, final celebration together.

Nancy found herself caught in a bittersweet moment when her beloved uncle passed away, marking the poignant interlude between her college graduation and the commencement of law school. Despite the sorrow that enveloped this period, it afforded her the opportunity to lend support to her grieving parents.

In the midst of mourning, she took charge of the intricate details involved in arranging her uncle's funeral, ensuring that the process unfolded with a seamless grace. One of the tasks she undertook was coordinating with a caterer to provide refreshments for the attendees, recognizing the importance of nurturing connections and shared moments of solace during the mourning process.

As she immersed herself in these responsibilities, she marveled at the multitude of people who gathered to pay their respects to her departed uncle. The outpouring of support from friends, extended family, and community members spoke volumes about the impact he had made on the lives of those around him.

In the midst of sorrow, Nancy found a sense of purpose in facilitating a dignified farewell for her uncle. The congregation of mourners became a testament to the profound influence he had wielded, leaving an indelible mark on the hearts of many who came to share their condolences.

Ginger and Danny arrived fashionably late for the church service, their presence adding a subtle sense of relief to the solemn occasion. Despite their tardiness, they managed to make it just in time for the poignant ceremony at the graveyard. Ginger, demonstrating a thoughtful gesture, wore a tasteful black dress that resonated with the somber atmosphere, eliciting gratitude from Nancy's mom and dad.

The air was heavy with grief as they joined the congregation gathered at the gravesite. The priest's words echoed through the stillness, offering solace and reflections on a life well-lived. The muted tones of sorrow mingled with the rustling of leaves, creating a poignant backdrop to the farewell for a beloved uncle.

Ginger and Danny, though arriving late, seamlessly integrated into the somber proceedings. Their presence was a testament to the enduring support that family and friends provide during times of loss. The graveyard commencement became a collective moment of reflection and closure, and Ginger's choice of attire added a touch of grace to the occasion, symbolizing respect for the solemnity of the event.

As Danny and Ginger moved through the crowd, attending to the refreshments and bidding farewell to departing guests, they seized a moment to approach Nancy away from the prying ears of his parents. In a hushed conversation, Danny couldn't help but address the pressing matter that had been lingering in his mind.

"When do they plan to go over the will?" Danny asked, his tone a mixture of impatience and a calculated practicality. "The faster that is done, the faster Mom and Dad can sell the cabin and acreage."

Nancy, caught off guard by the blunt inquiry, felt a surge of shock and anger. The weight of her brother's words struck a nerve, and she couldn't conceal her dismay. "You're a piece of work," she retorted, her words dripping with a blend of disbelief and frustration, before turning away and walking off.

The tension underscored the divergent perspectives within the family during this time of mourning. Danny's pragmatic approach clashed with Nancy's emotional response, emphasizing the delicate balance between grieving a loss and navigating the practicalities that follow.

In the aftermath of the funeral, the somber air settled over the family, and Nancy, along with her parents, found themselves facing the inevitable task of addressing Uncle Frank's estate. A meeting was convened to go over the details, with a clear emphasis on one specific aspect—no one was to enter the workshop, a space that held sentimental value and whispered secrets of Uncle Frank's craftsmanship.

The atmosphere in the room was tinged with a mix of grief and curiosity as Nancy's parents, resolute in their decision, did not extend an invitation to Danny for the review of the trust. It was a choice made in consideration of the potential complications that might arise, given Danny's previous inquiries about the will and the hasty disposition of the property.

As they delved into the details of Uncle Frank's estate, Nancy's parents acknowledged the weight of the decision ahead. Contrary to Danny's eager anticipation, they agreed that selling the cabin immediately might not be the wisest course of action. Instead, they entertained the idea of transforming the cabin into their permanent residence—a decision that would allow the legacy of Uncle Frank to endure in the very place he had poured his heart and soul into.

The family's dynamics shifted as they navigated the intricacies of grief, financial decisions, and the preservation of memories. The cabin, once a backdrop for shared family moments, now held the potential to become a permanent sanctuary, preserving the essence of Uncle Frank's spirit in every corner. Yet, as they moved forward, a lingering question remained—how would Danny respond to being excluded from the discussion and the potential change in plans for the cherished family cabin?

Several weeks elapsed, during which Nancy navigated the demanding challenges of law school. The cabin, once a haven crafted by Uncle Frank, stood silent and unoccupied as the promise of summer drew near. Nancy, seeking solace and a respite from the intensity of her studies, had already conveyed to her parents the end of her relationship with Ted.

She expressed her intention to spend the upcoming summer break at Uncle Frank's cabin, a decision motivated by a desire to reconnect with the memories and tranquility that the rustic retreat offered.

In light of this, Nancy's parents found themselves revisiting the idea of inviting Danny into the discussions about the estate. Recognizing the need for transparency and acknowledging the inevitable complexities that would arise, they came to the conclusion that it was time to address the matters surrounding Uncle Frank's legacy with him. The prospect of involving Danny was met with a mixture of trepidation and a determination to face whatever consequences might emerge.

The family acknowledged the delicate nature of these conversations, recognizing that the decisions made in the coming weeks would shape the future of the cabin and the legacy left behind by Uncle Frank. As they prepared to engage in these discussions, an undercurrent of uncertainty lingered—how would Danny react to being included, and what would be the ultimate fate of the cherished family cabin?

In that particular summer, mere months after the passing of Uncle Frank, Nancy embarked on a leisurely drive from her university's campus to the cherished cabin. The journey was imbued with a sense of nostalgia, as she marveled at the ever-changing landscape surrounding the cabin. Once blanketed in the pristine white of Christmas snow, the acreage had undergone a breathtaking transformation into lush green fields adorned with a vibrant array of wildflowers.

As Nancy approached, the focal point of the property became evident—the expansive pond that gracefully separated the main cabin from the adjacent garage. The tranquil waterbody played host to an enchanting assortment of migratory birds, their melodious calls serving as a harmonious announcement of her impending arrival. The symphony of avian greetings echoed through the air, reaching her parents who emerged from the cabin, eager to welcome her back to this haven of familial warmth. The reunion was set against the backdrop of the picturesque scene, epitomizing the timeless beauty of the cabin and its natural surroundings.

Following warm hugs and affectionate kisses, Nancy inquired about the anticipated arrival of her brother. "He mentioned he'd be joining us," her father responded. "Come inside, and let's go over the details of what your mom and I need to discuss. We're bracing ourselves for the possibility that Danny might react strongly, but it's unavoidable. Perhaps you can help us brainstorm a more effective strategy for conveying this to him."

Once inside the familiar confines of the cabin, the family gathered in the cozy living room. Nancy's parents exchanged glances that conveyed both the seriousness of the impending conversation and a shared determination to navigate it as smoothly as possible. The rustic ambiance of the cabin provided a comforting backdrop to the impending discussion.

As they settled into the worn-in furniture, Nancy's mother began outlining the delicate matter at hand, emphasizing the need for sensitivity and understanding. It was a topic laden with potential emotional turbulence, and they recognized the importance of approaching it with care. The family collectively brainstormed potential approaches, considering various angles and perspectives to ensure that Danny would comprehend the situation without undue distress.

In this intimate setting, the family unity and shared concern for Danny's well-being created a supportive atmosphere. The air was thick with the weight of the impending revelation, but together they forged a plan, hoping that Nancy's insight and familial bond would contribute to a smoother transition for her brother.

The unmistakable honking of Canadian geese marked both the arrival of Danny and the rumbling approach of his well-worn car. As the family gathered on the porch, they couldn't help but notice the familiar sight of Danny stepping out of his vehicle, accompanied by his girlfriend, Ginger.

Surveying the scene, Nancy's mom couldn't suppress a wry smile. "Looks like we're in for quite an interesting afternoon," she remarked, her eyes twinkling with a mix of anticipation and a touch of amusement. Recognizing the potential for a somewhat unpredictable encounter, she proposed a strategy to set a positive tone for the gathering.

"I think I will lay out a spread of food? It might be a good idea to let everyone enjoy lunch first and perhaps break the ice a bit," Nancy's mom suggested, the practicality of her suggestion evident in her tone. The notion of sharing a meal as a prelude to more serious discussions seemed like a sensible way to foster a relaxed atmosphere.

Nancy and her father warmly welcomed Danny and Ginger as the quartet strolled into the inviting cabin. The air outside carried the warmth of the day, and Ginger, seemingly unfazed by the occasion, had chosen a casual and relaxed ensemble. As they crossed the threshold into the cabin, Nancy couldn't help but reflect on what her late Uncle Frank might have quipped about Ginger's choice of attire, her thoughts drifting to the image of him playfully commenting on Ginger displaying more skin than a Main Street hooker.

Inside the cozy cabin, the atmosphere was a blend of familial warmth and a subtle undercurrent of curiosity. The rustic charm of the surroundings contrasted with the modernity Ginger brought with her, creating a dynamic that seemed to encapsulate the diverse elements of the family gathering. Nancy's mom stopped momentarily to welcome her son and Ginger and then returned to playing rolls and condiments on the kitchen table.

Nancy's dad, ever the gracious host, steered the group towards the living area, where the aroma of a freshly prepared meal wafted through the air. The family, enveloped in a mix of nostalgia and the present moment, settled into the comforting embrace of well-worn furniture. Nancy observed the interplay of personalities, realizing that the day held the promise of both lighthearted moments and potentially more serious discussions.

As the family bustled about, arranging a delightful array of dishes on the outdoor table, the aroma of home-cooked delights wafted through the air. The welcoming setup created a visual feast, with an assortment of colors and flavors awaiting their guests. The hope lingered in the air that this culinary gesture would serve as a unifying force, softening the potential tension of the impending conversation and paving the way for a more open and understanding exchange.

13

The atmosphere in the kitchen was thick with tension as Nancy, Danny, Ginger, and their parents sat around the worn wooden table, devouring sandwiches while an unspoken anticipation hung in the air. Nancy's parents, aware of the imminent storm, exchanged glances, the weight of their decision palpable. The cabin, once a symbol of shared memories, was now a potential source of familial discord.

Nancy's father took a deep breath, breaking the uneasy silence. "There's something we need to discuss," he began, the gravity of his words settling over the room. The revelation loomed as he explained that he and Danny's mom had decided to make the cabin their permanent retirement home instead of selling the property.

The announcement was met with a palpable shift in the room, the subtle intake of breath signaling Danny's brewing discontent.

As the tension reached its peak, Nancy's father produced an envelope, his attempt to soften the blow. "Your Uncle Frank left you both something," he said, passing the envelopes containing $10,000 each. The unexpected windfall did little to quell Danny's mounting frustration, but Nancy's father continued, detailing the future plans. They intended to create a new will and trust, allowing Danny and Nancy to decide the fate of the cabin after their parents' passing.

However, Danny, already seething, demanded answers about the workshop, a separate entity on a different deed. He questioned why it couldn't be sold for a larger inheritance. Nancy's mother interjected, explaining Uncle Frank's explicit wish that the workshop remain untouched, allowing nature to reclaim it over the years. The revelation only fueled Danny's anger.

In a moment of heated defiance, Danny snatched the envelopes containing the cash, a tangible representation of the family's complex dynamics. With Ginger by his side, he stormed out of the cabin, leaving behind the weight of unresolved emotions and the echoes of a familial rift. The door swung shut, a symbolic barrier closing on a chapter of shared history, leaving Nancy and her parents to grapple with the fallout of a decision that had shattered the fragile unity of their family.

Fuming with frustration, Danny settled into his car, determined to express his disdain for the recent turn of events. He pressed down on the accelerator, propelling the vehicle forward at a rapid speed, leaving the cabin behind in a blur. The wheels churned up dust along the winding path around the pond, startling the resident birds into a cacophony of loud, protesting calls.

As the engine roared and the landscape whizzed past, Danny couldn't contain his exasperation. "Can you believe that?" he vented, his tone laced with disappointment. "I had high hopes of learning that my uncle had left me with hundreds of thousands of dollars. I mean, I thought my parents were going to announce that they were putting the cabin and acreage up for sale, and we'd discuss how the money from the sale would be divided. Instead, I get this stupid $10,000. Once again, my skinflint uncle screwed me over."

The bitterness in Danny's voice echoed through the car, each word a testament to the shattered expectations that now lingered in the air. The speedometer climbed as he navigated the terrain, the outside world blurring into a manifestation of his internal turmoil. The disappointment of unmet financial expectations mingled with the sting of familial betrayal, leaving Danny to grapple with the harsh reality of the situation as he sped away, leaving behind the once-cherished family cabin and the bitter taste of perceived injustice.

"This isn't the end of it. I bet my sister had something to do with this. I'll consult with a lawyer and explore if there's any way I can challenge this decision," Danny declared with a steely resolve.

Ginger, ever the voice of reason, countered, "Danny, legal battles can be expensive. It might end up costing you more than the $10,000 you've got in your pocket." Despite her practical advice, Danny remained silent, his determination evident in his clenched jaw. As he confronted the winding road leading away from his uncle's property, he decided to ease off the accelerator, contemplating the tumultuous journey that lay ahead both literally and figuratively.

Armed with $10,000, Danny and Ginger opted for a night at a charming motel situated conveniently close to a fast-food joint, ensuring they had a place to grab dinner and breakfast. settling into their room, Danny wasted no time. He flipped through the phone book, dialing several attorneys in a quest for advice.

Unfortunately, only two attorneys agreed to a brief free consultation over the phone. Both conveyed a unanimous verdict: Danny had little to no recourse unless there was a mistake in the construction of the trust. Disheartened, Danny realized there was no such error, further fueling his frustration and causing him to seethe with resentment toward his deceased uncle. The night, instead of offering solace, became a battleground for Danny's internal turmoil.

In the swift passage of months, Nancy honed her study routine at law school, discovering it to be a more manageable endeavor than she initially anticipated. Regular phone calls to her parents painted a picture of significant changes on the home front – they had successfully sold their house and were gradually transitioning their belongings to the cabin while navigating the intricacies of the escrow process. The once-familiar surroundings of their long-time residence were being exchanged for the rustic charm of the cabin, a symbol of familial unity and shared history.

However, amid the whirlwind of adjustments, a notable absence loomed in the form of Danny. Neither Nancy nor her parents had heard a word from him, his silence creating an unspoken void within the family dynamic. The concern was palpable, and Nancy found herself grappling with a mix of emotions as she juggled the demands of law school and the uncertainty surrounding her brother's whereabouts.

The steady rhythm of Nancy's academic pursuits contrasted sharply with the unanswered questions surrounding Danny's actions. As she delved into her legal studies, a growing sense of detachment from her family's ongoing saga manifested. The cabin, once a beacon of cherished memories, now stood as a backdrop to a narrative marked by unresolved tensions and a conspicuous absence. The phone calls, once a lifeline to familial updates, became tinged with an unspoken longing for Danny's reentry into the fold, a hope that lingered on the periphery of Nancy's burgeoning legal career.

Opting to spend Thanksgiving at the university, Nancy found herself immersed in a sea of law-related assignments, as if all her professors collectively agreed to load her up with homework over the holiday break. The decision to stay on campus turned out to be fortuitous, considering the frenetic activity back at the cabin.

The day preceding Thanksgiving marked the culmination of her parents' final move to the cabin, and the atmosphere there was nothing short of chaotic. The monumental task of relocating four decades' worth of accumulated belongings from their former house to the cabin presented a formidable challenge. Despite the evident chaos, Nancy's mom and dad viewed this upheaval as an opportunity to declutter their lives, deciding to purge items that no longer served a purpose.

The process of packing and sorting became a journey through the memories encapsulated in each item, a reflective exercise tinged with nostalgia and practicality. The cabin, already a repository of family history, was now absorbing the physical remnants of a lifetime, creating a backdrop for a poignant chapter in the family's story.

As Nancy navigated the demands of her law studies during the holiday, she couldn't help but feel a sense of connection to the transformative events occurring at the cabin, a place that had not only witnessed the evolution of her family but was now undergoing its own metamorphosis.

As Christmas approached, the anticipation in the air at Uncle Frank's cabin took on a distinctly different hue. Nancy's parents had extended an olive branch, reaching out to Danny, and after a thoughtful period of consideration, he had accepted the invitation to join the family for the holiday festivities.

The news injected a renewed sense of hope and warmth into the cabin, transforming it into a beacon of familial unity once more. Nancy, balancing her law studies with the excitement of the impending reunion, couldn't help but feel a blend of joy and trepidation. The prospect of a family Christmas, with all its traditions and shared memories, carried a weight of expectations and the promise of healing.

Preparations for the festive season unfolded against the backdrop of the cabin's rustic charm. Decorations adorned the familiar spaces, blending with the nostalgia of past celebrations. The air was infused with the scent of pine from the freshly cut Christmas tree, standing proudly in the corner of the living room. Nancy's parents, embodying the spirit of the season, worked together to create a welcoming atmosphere, their efforts reflecting a genuine desire to reconnect as a family.

As the day drew near, Nancy couldn't help but wonder how the reunion would unfold. The cabin, a witness to both joyous and tumultuous moments, stood ready to embrace the latest chapter in the family's story. With the prospect of Danny's return, the once-fractured bonds seemed poised for mending, and the upcoming Christmas held the promise of restoration and newfound closeness.

Four days ahead of her brother's anticipated arrival, Nancy excitedly made her way to the cabin, eager to immerse herself in the preparations for the upcoming Christmas celebration. The prospect of reuniting with her family and reviving the festive spirit within the familiar walls filled her with anticipation.

Upon arriving, she wasted no time in joining her parents in adorning the cabin with festive decorations, inside and out. The scent of pine needles and the warm glow of twinkling lights began to transform the rustic space into a holiday haven. As they worked together, laughter and shared memories mingled with the rustle of wrapping paper and the hum of Christmas carols playing softly in the background.

In quiet moments, Nancy found herself stealing glances towards the garage, a place that held a trove of nostalgic memories. In her mind's eye, she could envision her late uncle, hidden away in his secret man cave, passionately whittling away at his creations. The image of him emerging, covered in a fine layer of wood chips, added a touch of bittersweet nostalgia to the holiday preparations. The garage, once a sanctuary of creativity, now stood as a silent tribute to Uncle Frank's unique spirit, a presence that lingered in the air, infusing the festive season with a sense of continuity.

As Nancy and her parents continued their decorating efforts, the cabin transformed into a festive refuge, each ornament and strand of lights contributing to the creation of cherished holiday memories. The anticipation of Danny's arrival added an extra layer of warmth to the preparations, and the cabin, once again, became a place where family bonds were nurtured and the spirit of Christmas flourished.

"So, any ideas on how we're going to pull this off?" inquired Ginger, her curiosity piqued.

With a sardonic smirk, Danny responded, "We'll make a grand entrance, armed with balls of holly and wear the jolliest smiles you've ever seen, as if all is forgiven. Picture it - a regular holiday cheer extravaganza. But here's the catch: like the Grinch who stole Christmas, once we've fooled them all, we'll make our way to the workshop and break in. And don't let me forget to grab those bags from the trunk; we'll need them to carry my uncle's creations. If we manage to execute this covert operation without anyone catching on, we quietly retreat to our car and hightail it out of here."

The plan unfolded in Danny's words, a risky scheme veiled in humor and subterfuge. The festive façade of holly and smiles would serve as their Trojan horse, concealing the clandestine mission to retrieve Uncle Frank's cherished creations. The workshop, a realm of memories and artistic endeavors, would become the focal point of their Christmas caper, a venture both daring and emotionally charged. The bags, waiting in the trunk, symbolized the tangible connection they sought to maintain with Uncle Frank's legacy.

As Danny outlined the plan to Ginger, the gravity of their mission became apparent. The cabin, aglow with holiday decorations and the laughter of family, would unwittingly host a clandestine operation, with the two of them navigating the delicate balance between deception and preserving the memory of a beloved uncle. The success of their venture rested on executing the plan with Grinch-like precision and evading detection as they carried out this bittersweet holiday heist.

In a well-rehearsed display of familial affection, Danny and Ginger gracefully exchanged hugs and kisses with everyone upon stepping into the warm embrace of the cabin. Effortlessly, they seamlessly wove their way into the festive atmosphere, their arrival marked by genuine compliments about the impeccably adorned interiors and the captivating display of holiday decorations that adorned the exterior. The air was saturated with the enticing aromas wafting from the kitchen, where the promise of a delightful Christmas feast awaited.

Nancy and her parents, their excitement hard to contain, couldn't help but notice the transformative shift in Danny's demeanor. His once unmistakable tension seemed to dissipate, replaced by a more congenial spirit that mirrored the joyous ambiance of the holiday season. The sight of Danny's newfound cheer brought smiles to their faces, a welcomed change that hinted at the possibility of healing and reconnection.

Yet, amid the celebration, there lingered a subtle concern about Ginger's choice of attire, a detail that seemed to have changed little. While Danny's transformation was evident, the same couldn't be said for Ginger, who still carried an air of inappropriate dress. The dissonance between the festive setting and Ginger's attire became a minor discord in the overall harmonious scene, a detail that caught the observant eyes of Nancy and her parents.

As the cabin buzzed with the shared joy of the season, Danny and Ginger's entrance became a pivotal moment, a delicate balance between embracing the holiday cheer and addressing the nuances that hinted at underlying tensions. The challenge lay in navigating this festive façade while holding onto the hope that the reunion would, in fact, be a catalyst for healing and renewed family bonds.

Feigning the need to retreat to their room for a festive task of wrapping presents, Danny and Ginger tactfully excused themselves from the lively atmosphere of the cabin. The pretext, draped in the holiday spirit, granted them a moment of seclusion to carry out a clandestine operation. Once behind the closed door of their room, Danny swiftly unzipped his suitcase, revealing a stash of bags containing something unconventional—coal.

Carefully, Danny extracted the bags, each lump of coal encased in protective bubble wrap. He reached for festive cans, transforming the traditionally symbolic containers into vessels of unexpected surprise. With meticulous precision, he placed the bubble-wrapped coal inside, each can a deceptive package of yuletide cheer. The labels on the cans were adorned with holiday flair, disguising the unexpected contents within.

Danny's covert mission took a mischievous turn as he embarked on an unconventional Christmas gift-giving endeavor. The cans, one addressed to his mom, another for his dad, and the last destined for his sister, became unsuspecting carriers of a playful prank. The element of surprise, disguised in the festive wrapping, added a layer of humor to an otherwise ordinary Christmas tradition. "Let's see how they like receiving coal as a Christmas gift," he said as the two made their way downstairs to the Christmas tree.

As Danny and Ginger engaged in this holiday mischief, the unsuspecting family members downstairs continued to revel in the joy of the season. Little did they know that beneath the veneer of holiday cheer, a whimsical scheme was unfolding in the confines of Danny and Ginger's room, setting the stage for an unexpected twist in the Christmas celebration.

Nancy's mom showcased her culinary prowess by preparing a delectable homemade spaghetti, a dish she took immense pride in crafting. As the tantalizing aroma wafted through the cabin, it became evident that a labor of love was unfolding in the kitchen. Meanwhile, Nancy, eager to contribute to the feast, assembled a basket filled with aromatic garlic breadsticks, accompanied by a freshly tossed salad complete with a flavorful dressing.

The air in the cabin became saturated with the enticing scents of the impending meal. The rich aroma of simmering spaghetti sauce, the warm notes of freshly baked garlic bread, and the crisp freshness of the salad collectively created a symphony of flavors that promised a delightful culinary experience. The inviting tableau set the stage for a communal gathering, where the anticipation for the upcoming feast heightened with each passing moment.

Even Danny and Ginger, known for their candidness, couldn't help but express their genuine excitement. The enticing smells emanating from the kitchen elicited honest comments about their eagerness to indulge in the savory spread that awaited them. The prospect of savoring Nancy's mom's homemade spaghetti, complemented by the delectable sides, stirred a shared sentiment of anticipation among the family members.

As they all gathered around the table, the atmosphere buzzed with the collective joy of a shared meal. The culmination of culinary efforts and the aroma of home-cooked goodness created a moment that went beyond mere sustenance—it was a celebration of family, tradition, and the simple pleasures of coming together around a table filled with delicious food.

Danny and Ginger, signaling the end of the evening's festivities, were the first to express their intention to call it a night. "Big day ahead tomorrow," Danny announced with a hint of enthusiasm. Ginger chimed in, "Yeah, we need to hit the hay so Santa can work his magic," playfully swiping a few cookies before the two made their way to their room.

Observing their departure, Nancy's mom couldn't help but remark on the noticeable transformation in Danny's demeanor. "He's like a whole new person," she marveled, her surprise evident in her voice.

"It's the season, Mom," Nancy reassured her. "This time of year has a way of bringing out the best in people. Maybe my brother has finally come to terms with the way things are and is ready to move forward with his life. Although, I still can't quite figure out what he's searching for."

Curiosity piqued, her dad inquired, "What do you mean?"

Nancy continued, "He still doesn't have a steady job. I can't fathom how anyone manages to get by without medical care, and I have my doubts about whether he even has automobile insurance. And then there's Ginger. I hate to say it, but what does he see in her? She once mentioned she had a scholarship to a four-year college, majoring in business. When I asked why she didn't finish, she told me her dad passed away, and she just lost all motivation. That's when she found Danny."

The revelations about Ginger's past painted a complex picture, adding layers to the mystery of Danny's choices. As the family dispersed for the night, Nancy couldn't shake the questions lingering in her mind, contemplating the uncertainties that surrounded her brother's decisions and the enigma that was Ginger.

Nancy's mom hesitated for a moment before sharing a memory that had lingered in her mind. "You know," she began, "your uncle once made a comment about Ginger that, at the time, I thought was just one of his sarcastic quips. He mentioned that, with her intelligence and beauty, she could have been a corporate executive." She paused, a thoughtful expression crossing her face. "I chuckled when he said it."

The revelation cast a new light on Ginger's background, introducing a layer of complexity to the perception of her. Nancy's mom, having initially dismissed Uncle Frank's remark as a jest, now found herself reconsidering its potential sincerity. The notion that Ginger, despite her current circumstances, might have had the potential for a different path hinted at untold facets of her life.

As the family gathered around, the revelation sparked a reflective silence. Uncle Frank's words, once regarded as mere banter, took on a new significance. The mystery surrounding Ginger's choices and the divergent paths she could have taken added a sense of intrigue to the family dynamic. The cabin, already brimming with history and untold stories, seemed to hold more secrets than they had initially realized.

Nancy's dad, his gaze fixed on the dancing flames in the fireplace, broke the contemplative silence with a reflective admission. "No parent wishes for their son to go off to war, but looking back, I think my brother had a point when he believed that Danny should have enlisted in the Armed Forces," he acknowledged. The crackling fire seemed to echo the seriousness of the conversation.

His expression held a mixture of regret and self-reflection as he continued, "I suppose I didn't do a very good job of teaching him how to be a man – instilling the importance of setting goals and actively pursuing them. The military could have provided him with that sense of direction. Who knows, maybe he would have found fulfillment in military life and made it a career. Even if not, the experience could have equipped him with invaluable life skills that might have guided him towards a more purposeful career path."

The warmth of the fire provided a stark contrast to the weightiness of the topic at hand. The flickering flames seemed to illuminate the missed opportunities and the potential paths that diverged from Danny's current trajectory. The contemplation of what might have been added a layer of poignancy to the family's shared history, as they collectively reflected on the untrodden roads that could have shaped Danny's journey in a different way.

17

Danny's gaze fell on his wristwatch, the luminous hands indicating the solitude of 2:30 in the morning. Straining his ears, he detected no sounds emanating from the cabin's sleeping depths. He gently shook Ginger awake, his urgency conveyed in a hushed tone. "It's time. Gather your things; we won't be returning here," he whispered.

In a matter of moments, the duo moved with stealthy precision, descending the stairs as if navigating a labyrinth of silence. Every step was a calculated dance, avoiding creaky floor joints that threatened to betray their covert departure. The shadows cloaked them, and the silence of the night held an unspoken agreement with their clandestine exit.

The air outside was crisp, and the surroundings took on an ethereal glow in the moonlit night. The cabin, nestled in the quietude of the sleeping woods, became a backdrop to their surreptitious departure. The urgency in Danny's actions hinted at the weight of their decision—leaving the cabin behind, perhaps for good. The initial crunching of the snow caused them to stop their advance towards the garage, but they both realized those sounds could not be heard in the cabin.

As they ventured into the night, the only sounds were the muted whispers of the wind and the soft crunch of snow beneath their footsteps. The landscape unfolded like a tableau, each step marking the end of one chapter and the uncertain beginning of another. The stillness of the night held the echoes of their departure, a departure that left the cabin to bask in the solitude of the night, unaware of the quiet exit that had transpired within its walls.

Bathed in the gentle glow of the moon, the structure housing the coveted treasures stood before them. Danny, gripping a flashlight in the darkness, shared a plan to navigate the situation. "My mom mentioned that the power is still on, so once we're inside, we won't need these flashlights. Let's circle around to the back. We can force the lock on the rear door," he instructed with a determined hush, the urgency of their mission reflected in his words.

The moonlight cast elongated shadows as they cautiously made their way around the perimeter. Each step carried a weight of anticipation, and the mere thought of what lay inside the structure heightened the palpable tension. The structure, once a repository of cherished memories, now harbored the allure of elusive treasures that Danny and Ginger sought.

As they reached the rear of the building, the cover of darkness provided a shroud for their clandestine activities. Danny, with a practiced hand, produced the necessary tools to address the locked door. The crisp night air carried a sense of suspense as the duo worked to gain access, the metallic clicks of their efforts muffled by the stillness of the night.

After determined efforts the door yielded, swinging open. Danny remembered where the light switch was and flipped it on revealing the interior bathed in a faint glow from the powered lights within. The need for flashlights dissipated as they stepped into a realm that held the echoes of Uncle Frank's creativity.

To their astonishment, the space was not just a garage; it was a treasure trove of Uncle Frank's craftsmanship. The air was thick with the scent of wood, the tangible manifestation of countless hours spent creating handmade toys.

The sheer magnitude of the workshop's contents left Danny and Ginger momentarily speechless. Row upon row of meticulously crafted toys lined the shelves, each a testament to Uncle Frank's passion for woodworking. The workshop, a space that had once seemed small and unassuming, now expanded into a realm of creativity and nostalgia.

Danny's eyes widened as he took in the sight of toy soldiers standing at attention, wooden cars lined up with precision, and dolls with intricately painted faces. Ginger, her hand over her mouth in awe, marveled at the delicate craftsmanship evident in every piece.

The workshop, which had been a secret sanctuary for Uncle Frank, now revealed its hidden wonders to his nephew and his companion.

In the hushed atmosphere of the workshop, Danny and Ginger moved reverently through the space, the florescent lights illuminating the handmade wonders that surrounded them. The realization dawned that Uncle Frank's passion for crafting toys had transcended mere hobby; it had been a labor of love, a dedication to spreading joy through his art.

As they explored further, uncovering the depths of Uncle Frank's creative legacy, Danny and Ginger felt a profound connection to the man who had left such a lasting imprint on their lives. The workshop, once shrouded in secrecy, now became a sacred space of discovery, weaving a poignant narrative of familial bonds and the enduring power of handmade creations.

The transformation in Ginger was magical. The skepticism and uncertainty that had clouded her eyes in the earlier moments gave way to a softness, a vulnerability that spoke of a connection to a cherished past. The doll, now a symbol of unfulfilled childhood dreams and the enduring spirit of Christmas, had a profound impact on Ginger's demeanor.

As Ginger and Danny continued to explore the enchanting workshop, Ginger's eyes suddenly caught a glimmer of something familiar on one of the shelves. Amidst the myriad of handcrafted wonders, there it was—a delicate doll with porcelain features and a gown adorned with intricate lace. A surge of emotions washed over Ginger as she recognized the doll she had longed for as a small girl, fervently believing in the magic of Christmas.

She reached out and delicately cradled the doll in her hands, her fingers tracing the intricate details that Uncle Frank had bestowed upon it. The memories of her childhood flooded back, bringing with them the innocence and joy of a time when she had eagerly awaited Santa's visit. Ginger's eyes glistened with a mix of nostalgia and gratitude as she held the cherished doll, a tangible link to a Christmas dream that had once felt unattainable.

The transformation in Ginger was magical. The skepticism and uncertainty that had clouded her eyes in the earlier moments gave way to a softness, a vulnerability that spoke of a connection to a cherished past. The doll, now a symbol of unfulfilled childhood dreams and the enduring spirit of Christmas, had a profound impact on Ginger's demeanor.

In that quiet moment within the workshop, surrounded by Uncle Frank's creations, Ginger felt a profound shift within herself. The rediscovery of the doll became a poignant reminder of the enduring magic that Christmas held, even in the midst of life's complexities. The workshop, once a space of mystery and clandestine activities, now witnessed a personal transformation unfolding as Ginger, with the cherished doll in her hands, found herself rekindling a belief in the enchantment of the holiday season.

With the delicate doll cradled in the embrace of both her arms, Ginger felt an inexplicable sense of connection and comfort. It was as if, in that moment, the cherished doll held the power to erase the memories of her tumultuous past and the dysfunctional Christmas traditions that had once haunted her. The weight of those recollections seemed to dissipate, slipping through her grasp like sand escaping between her fingers. Her tears continued to follow down her cheeks.

As Ginger attempted to summon memories of her family's dysfunction and the Christmases tainted by discord, she found an unexpected veil settling over those recollections. Try as she might, the images of strained relationships and fractured festivities eluded her grasp. It was as though the mere presence of the doll had ushered in a transformative magic, gently guiding her thoughts away from the shadows of the past.

A perplexing realization dawned upon Ginger as she questioned herself internally, contemplating the unusual shift in her perception. "What is happening to me?" she wondered aloud, her voice a mere whisper in the hushed workshop. In response, a wave of warmth, love, and glee surged through her being, overwhelming any lingering doubts or uncertainties.

In the gentle glow of Uncle Frank's workshop, Ginger's metamorphosis unfolded. The doll, once a symbol of childhood dreams, now seemed to radiate a transformative energy that infused her with newfound positivity. The barriers of skepticism and past grievances melted away, replaced by an embrace of warmth, love, and the genuine joy that Christmas could bring. Ginger, in the quiet sanctuary of the workshop, experienced a profound shift—a release from the shackles of the past and an emergence into a moment of genuine happiness and unexpected enchantment.

Concern etched across his face, Danny approached Ginger, his voice filled with worry. "What's wrong? Are you hurt?" he inquired, noting the tears streaming down her face.

Ginger, still clutching the doll close to her chest, struggled to find the right words. "I... I don't know," she confessed, her voice tinged with a mixture of bewilderment and joy. "I feel like I'm floating, like I've been enveloped in some kind of enchantment. I'm so overwhelmingly happy, and it scares me."

As the words escaped Ginger's lips, a sense of vulnerability hung in the air. The unexpected surge of happiness and the surreal feeling of being under an emotional spell left her grappling with a cascade of conflicting emotions. The doll, nestled against her, seemed to be a conduit for this inexplicable transformation, weaving an unexpected thread of magic into the fabric of the moment.

Danny, now more puzzled than ever, tried to comprehend the mysterious turn of events. Ginger's tears, usually associated with sorrow, now mirrored a blend of joy and trepidation. In the quiet expanse of Uncle Frank's workshop, the atmosphere seemed charged with an otherworldly energy, as though the dolls and toys crafted with love were imparting a magic that extended beyond the realm of mere craftsmanship. The unfolding scene left Danny and Ginger suspended between the mundane and the magical, grappling with emotions that defied easy explanation.

"Damn, there's an overwhelming amount of stuff in here. We won't be able to clear it all out," Danny muttered, refocusing on the task at hand. As he surveyed the workshop, his attention was drawn to a particular spot. There it was, lying alone on top of a substantial binder cloaked in a layer of wood chips. It was a sight that instantly transported him back to a long-forgotten era—the pirate ship he had yearned for so earnestly in countless Christmases past.

In a perceptible moment of stillness, Danny's surroundings seemed to fade away. The usual symphony of sounds within the workshop ceased, the familiar scent of wood chips momentarily vanished, and even the presence of Ginger felt elusive. It was as if time itself had folded, and Danny found himself transported to the golden days spent alongside his uncle.

In this suspended moment, memories of shared laughter, the rhythmic melody of whittling, and the camaraderie that came with solving life's myriad problems flooded Danny's consciousness. The workshop, once a cavernous space filled with tangible creations, now became a vessel for time travel, ushering him back to those cherished moments of bonding with his uncle.

As he stood there, Danny envisioned himself in the very spot where he had forged numerous creations under the watchful guidance of his uncle. The echoes of shared wisdom, the easy banter that defined their relationship, and the tangible love he held for the man who stood as a beacon of guidance in his life resurfaced with vivid clarity.

The workshop, once bustling with the noise of crafting and the banter of kindred spirits, now held the silent whispers of nostalgia. It was a sanctuary where the craftsmanship of wood became a conduit for the transmission of lessons, laughter, and love. In this transient journey to the past, Danny rediscovered the profound impact his uncle had on shaping not just the tangible creations in the workshop but also the enduring fabric of his own character.

In a fleeting moment, the allure of the pirate ship temporarily slipped from Danny's thoughts, overshadowed by the sight of an object partially concealed by the sea-faring model. It was an unexpected find that stirred a wave of emotions within him. How could it still be here after all these years? He had thought it lost, or perhaps his uncle, in a moment of frustration, had sold it. The object itself didn't require an extensive display of whittling talent; his uncle had once shown him that the skill he had honed could bring it to life in less than 20 minutes.

The item in question was a diminutive Santa, standing at a mere 3 inches in height and measuring about 1 ½ inches in width. The base all coming from the same block of basswood. Despite its modest size, the wooden creation held immense sentimental value for Danny. Memories flooded back of his uncle cautioning him about the delicate nature of the creation, particularly the intricacies around Santa's eyes. It was a testament to the level of precision and care required in the art of whittling, a craft his uncle had painstakingly trained him in.

Danny's pride swelled as he recollected the hours spent sanding and meticulously painting the little Santa. The miniature masterpiece had garnered praise not only from his parents but also from his sister. It was a tangible representation of his growing proficiency in whittling, a skill that went beyond the creation itself to encompass the bond he shared with his uncle. In the quiet workshop, the rediscovery of the tiny Santa became a poignant thread connecting past achievements, familial approval, and the enduring legacy of the craft that had shaped Danny's hands and heart.

19

Danny was abruptly pulled back to the present by the sound of Ginger's voice. She was engrossed in a conversation with her doll, a spectacle that left him momentarily perplexed. "Are you okay? You look like you've seen a ghost," she quipped, attempting to stifle a laugh. "Hey, what's that? That is really cool."

In his hands, Danny held the tiny Santa, turning it around and tracing the familiar contours with his fingers. A flood of memories washed over him, each cut with his carving knife etched into the wooden figure. "I can't believe it. This was the first thing I ever learned to carve," he mused, a sense of nostalgia and accomplishment filling his words.

"No way. You carved this on your first try?" Ginger inquired, leaning in closely to inspect the intricacies of the miniature Santa after Danny handed it to her. The disbelief in her eyes mirrored the astonishment that Danny himself had experienced upon rediscovering the tiny masterpiece. The workshop, once a silent witness to the craft's evolution, now bore witness to a moment of shared revelation between Danny and Ginger—a testament to the enduring magic that could be found in the art of creation and the unexpected surprises that unfolded within the walls of Uncle Frank's workshop.

"Hey, what's that?" Ginger inquired, pointing at the binder that had momentarily slipped Danny's mind. He reached up and delicately lifted the pirate ship. "Man, that ship is beautiful. Did you carve that also?" Ginger asked, admiration evident in her gaze.

"No, that's the ship I told you about—the one I wanted so badly for Christmas. Like I said, my Uncle Frank was a gifted carver. Do you know how many hours went into this piece?" Danny posed the question rhetorically, not expecting an immediate answer. After carefully placing the ship in its designated spot, he settled down at a nearby table with the binder.

Blowing off the accumulated dust, Danny opened the first page, revealing a treasure trove of memories and sketches. Ginger, captivated by the unfolding narrative, took a seat beside him. The workshop, now a haven of rediscovery, witnessed the duo immersing themselves in the tales preserved within the pages of the binder—a chronicle of craftsmanship, dreams, and the enduring legacy of Uncle Frank's artistry.

"These are patterns he used to create all these toys. There are pages and pages here," Danny exclaimed, his excitement palpable. He reached a divider and turned the page, only to be met with something that truly blew him away.

"Hey, it looks like a letter," Ginger chimed in, her eyes alight with curiosity. "Who is it for?"

"It's addressed to me from Uncle Frank," Danny revealed, his voice carrying a mix of surprise and affection.

"Well, read it," Ginger urged, her impatience masked by a festive smile that reflected the joyful atmosphere lingering in the workshop. As Danny unfolded the contents of the letter, the words from Uncle Frank seemed to bridge the gap between past and present:

'Danny, my favorite and only nephew. I knew that you would be the one in the family unable to overcome the curiosity of the contents inside my workshop. I'm not mad, since at your age, I would have probably done the same. I bet your better half is with you also. Hi, Ginger.'

"Wow, that's spooky. Continue," Ginger insisted, her intrigue intensifying. The workshop, once a silent repository of craftsmanship, now echoed with the words of Uncle Frank, creating a poignant connection between generations and the enduring spirit of family bonds.

Danny smiled at Ginger noticing a change in her before continuing. 'You accused me and held it against me for so many years, that I withheld my earnings from the sale of my creations from you and the family. I'm about to reveal to you the true nature of the workshop the two of you have entered.'

Before your Aunt Susie passed away, I crafted exquisite wooden toys that I sold to various companies, earning a considerable amount of money. In times of hardship, I generously shared some of his earnings with Danny's parents, aiding them during tough financial stretches and contributing to Nancy's college tuition. However, you, Danny, took a divergent path, persistently rejecting academic pursuits, an enlistment in the military, and instead you chased get-rich-quick schemes, leading you into brushes with the law.'

The breaking point in our relationship occurred during a heated argument, resulting from me placing a lump of coal in your Christmas present. The tension between us became unbearable, and our once-close bond seemed irreparably damaged. Then, an unexpected epiphany reshaped my perspective.'

'During one routine day of delivering wooden toys to a business, a torn bag spilled its contents onto the sidewalk. A homeless woman and her daughter came to my aid, helping me collect the scattered items. The little girl's eyes lit up with joy upon seeing one of the dolls, and I decided to give it to her. The sheer excitement brought tears to the girl's eyes. In that moment, something shifted within me.

Overwhelmed by the emotional impact of giving my handmade creations to those less fortunate, I experienced a profound change. From that point forward, I transformed my approach to running the workshop. While I continued to sell toys to vendors, I now managed the funds separately, entrusting your parents with his trust upon my passing.

Simultaneously, a new venture unfolded. In addition to satisfying vendors, I started delivering toys to various charities. Moreover, I placed ads in publications, inviting struggling parents to send letters to "Santa" at the workshop. At my own expense, I crafted the requested toys and mailed them to families in need, embracing the spirit of giving that had ignited within me.'

'Pause on the writing for now, both of you. Head to the office near the bathroom, and we'll discover something," the words of Uncle Frank echoed in their minds, a directive that compelled Danny and Ginger to follow the instructions laid out in the letter.

Opening the office door, they were greeted by a cascade of letters addressed to the workshop, pouring out onto the floor in a voluminous display. "Oh, my God. Look at all of them," Ginger exclaimed, bending down to pick up a few letters and showing them to Danny.

True to Uncle Frank's description, each envelope bore the address to Santa, care of the workshop. The sight of the letters, a tangible manifestation of the heartfelt requests from families in need, left Danny and Ginger awe-struck, realizing the depth of Uncle Frank's clandestine venture to bring joy and warmth to those who reached out to Santa at the workshop.

20

Danny and Ginger hurriedly returned the letters to the room, stuffing them back inside, and closed the door with a resolute force before Danny resumed reading the letter. "As you two have now seen, I created a monster, but until my health really failed me, I loved being here in the workshop working on the dreams of so many unfortunate kids."

"Since you are reading this, I have gone to join your Aunt Susie, provided that God has forgiven my sins. So now, my nephew, I have a proposition. You have a talent as a carver. I saw it the first time you picked up a carving knife and looked at a block of wood. You are an artist; don't let it go to waste."

"I purposely placed the property this workshop stands on in a separate deed of trust. Inside this envelope is a card from my attorney. If you decide to act on what I am proposing, he will handle all the details. This also applies to you, Ginger."

"I would like for you not only to own but also manage the workshop, Danny. There are far too many objects to be made by hand for one craftsman. Instead, I would like you to hire and train craftsmen to help you not only handle the Santa letter requests but also to run the profit side of the business."

"Your job, Ginger, if you are up for it, is to use your business sense to assist with the operational side of the workshop. You will have to handle taxes, business licenses, mailing of products, and so on. For the legal aspects, you both should rely on your sister, Nancy.'

"Oh, and by the way, Ginger, take some of the money from my, no, Danny's business account and invest in some beautiful clothes to accentuate your natural beauty. You two are going to be running a multi-million-dollar business, so you have to look the part.'

'Now, this might sound overwhelming, and if you two try to handle it on your own, it will be, so let me outline what you should consider. First, take this letter and binder into the cabin. Wait for everyone to wake up on Christmas morning. Then, over your mom's Christmas buffet, lay it all out for them. Yes, I know your mom and dad will be upset, knowing you two broke into the workshop, but after you read this letter, they will understand."

'Next, take some of the money from the business account and hire someone to remodel part of the workshop into living quarters for the two of you. By the way, yes, I'm old school, so by golly, you two better get married, damn it. But, I digress. While the workshop is being remodeled, start hiring craftsmen to help with production. Don't forget to hire some novices that you can train, Danny."

'I'm guessing it is Christmas Day as you read this, so you must start working on the carving soon, since the next Christmas will be here before you know it."

'Finally, I want to apologize for the way I acted these last few years. The coal in the Christmas present idea was stupid on my part. You accused me of being a skinflint and tight with sharing my money. Now you know the truth. You two can become extremely wealthy with the business proposition I have presented to you, but I promise you, you will not lose the Christmas spirit that I hope you have now found in your hearts. Love, Uncle Frank.'

Tears welled up in Danny's eyes, and Ginger, too, wept in joy. After years of harboring dislike for his uncle's actions, Danny found himself inheriting not only a highly successful business but also a career that had ignited his passion in the past. The weight of resentment lifted, replaced by gratitude and a newfound appreciation for Uncle Frank's vision.

As for Ginger, basking in the accolades bestowed upon her by 'Uncle Frank' and relishing the challenge of running a business with Danny, she experienced a Christmas beyond belief. The glow of accomplishment and the unexpected turn of events infused her with a sense of purpose, propelling her into a role she hadn't envisioned but wholeheartedly embraced. Together, they stood on the threshold of a future filled with potential, both personally and professionally, a far cry from the uncertainty they had faced just moments before.

Danny carefully folded the letter, placing it at the front of the binder. As he did, the remaining three-fourths of its contents displayed addresses for charities, vendors, suppliers, and various shippers. Closing the binder, he looked over at Ginger. "My uncle was right about a lot of things. The most important one being that you and I should get married, if you'll have me."

"This has been the best Christmas ever for me," Ginger replied as she hugged and kissed Danny while holding her doll in her left arm.

"We need to head back to the cabin. I need to do a few things here first. Do you think you can find your way back yourself?" Danny asked.

"Sure. You don't need me here?" she asked.

"No. I just need a few minutes alone. You understand? I'll meet you in bed. Love ya."

21

Christmas morning unfolded with enchantment, bringing an air of magic that permeated the household. Nancy, eager to be the first one in the kitchen, was taken aback to discover not only her brother but also the presence of Ginger, a delightful surprise that added an extra layer of warmth to the festive atmosphere. The tantalizing aroma of freshly brewed coffee filled the air, complemented by an array of cookies and pastries meticulously arranged on the kitchen table by Ginger.

Noticing the early risers, Nancy couldn't resist teasingly inquiring, "Boy, you guys got up early. Couldn't sleep?"

Danny, with a mischievous smile, responded, "We had to check to see if Santa found the place."

Amused by Danny's playful remark, Nancy couldn't help but remark on the sudden surge of Christmas spirit. "Boy, someone has had the Christmas spirit the last few days. What's up with that?"

In a lighthearted tone, Danny quipped, "Hey, if it can happen to Ebenezer Scrooge, it can happen to anyone, right?" Ginger, playing the perfect host, offered Danny a cup of coffee.

Curious about Ginger's plans, Nancy inquired about her night's rest. "So how did you sleep, Ginger?"

Ginger, displaying a radiant smile, shared her exciting plans, "Oh, I slept great. I'm thinking of going back to business school next semester. I only have one more to do, and I will have my bachelor's. Who knows? I may even go on to grad school."

Encouraged by Ginger's ambitious goals, Nancy expressed her enthusiasm, "Wow, that would be wonderful."

As Nancy's parents joined the scene, the conversation shifted to Ginger's aspirations, earning her heartfelt congratulations. Danny's father, injecting humor, interjected with a request for breakfast, listing a tempting menu of pancakes, scrambled eggs, sausage, and hashbrowns.

Nancy's mother promptly took charge, and to everyone's surprise, Ginger offered to assist. Collaborating with Nancy, they seamlessly orchestrated a delightful breakfast, with Danny and his father contributing to the table-setting efforts. Laughter and shared stories filled the air, creating a joyful ambiance.

With satisfied appetites, Nancy's mother suggested moving to the grand room to commence the gift-opening festivities. When asked to play

Santa, Nancy, with a mischievous glint in her eye, nominated Ginger for the role, earning unanimous applause. Ginger, blushing but gracious, accepted the unexpected honor.

Amid the wrapping paper and festive cheer, Ginger, picking up the first gift, inadvertently revealed her initial hesitation. It turned out to be a present for Danny's father, containing a lump of coal. Recognizing her momentary embarrassment, Danny reassured her with a wink, "It's alright. He will love it." The room filled with laughter, epitomizing the true spirit of Christmas joy and shared moments with loved ones.

Carefully wrapped in festive paper, the anticipation in the room heightened as Danny watched his dad unwrap his intricately crafted wooden creation. With a twinkle in his eye, Danny explained, "Dad, I wanted to give you something special this year, something that comes straight from the heart."

As the wrapping paper was gently peeled away, a beautifully carved wooden sailing ship emerged. The level of detail was astonishing — each sail, rigging, and hull meticulously carved to perfection. The ship rested on a sturdy wooden base, showcasing Danny's dedication and skill in woodworking.

Nancy, Ginger, and the rest of the family were awe-struck by the craftsmanship. The sailing ship seemed to capture not only Danny's talent but also a profound connection to memories shared with his father, perhaps from their adventures or shared love for the sea.

With genuine surprise and admiration, Danny's father exclaimed, "Danny, this is incredible! Did you carve this yourself?"

Danny nodded proudly, "Yeah, I spent a few hours working on it, hoping to capture the spirit of our shared experiences. I know how much you love sailing, and I wanted to create something that reflects our bond."

The room was filled with a sense of warmth and appreciation as Danny's father carefully examined the hand-carved gift. The sailing ship, with its symbolic significance, became a cherished memento, embodying the love and thoughtfulness behind Danny's creation.

The family exchanged smiles, recognizing that sometimes, the most meaningful gifts are those that are crafted with time, dedication, and a deep understanding of the recipient's passions. Danny's hand-carved sailing ship stood not only as a testament to his artistic abilities but also as a symbol of the enduring bond between father and son, sailing through the seas of shared memories.

Danny's mom was next. After reading the tag on the present, Ginger again looked quizzically at Danny, remembering again that the original gift was supposed to be coal. She received another wink. All eyes were on Danny's mom as she opened the box containing her present.

Continuing with the theme of heartfelt handcrafted gifts, Danny turned his attention to his mom. With a gleam of excitement in his eyes, he watched her open a beautifully wrapped package, carefully concealing a hand-carved picture frame.

"Dad got the sailing ship, and I thought, Mom, you deserve something just as special," Danny said.

As the wrapping paper was gently removed, a stunning wooden picture frame emerged. The frame was a work of art in itself, adorned with intricate carvings that seemed to tell a story. Delicate patterns, reminiscent of vines and flowers, adorned the edges, creating a captivating border for any cherished photograph.

Nancy, Ginger, and the rest of the family were captivated by the craftsmanship, marveling at the attention to detail. The frame exuded a timeless elegance that perfectly complemented the precious memories it was meant to encase.

"Oh, Danny, this is truly enchanting!" exclaimed Danny's mom, her eyes aglow with delight. She swiftly crossed the room, embracing him with a heartfelt kiss and a warm hug.

"Mom! Don't go all Hallmark on me," a joking Danny replied.

"Alright, I'll be genuinely disappointed if I don't uncover one of your magical creations inside," Nancy chimed in, her anticipation evident as she eagerly accepted the present handed to her by Ginger.

As she carefully unwrapped the gift, Nancy felt a sense of intrigue building within her. The paper crinkled, revealing a meticulously crafted cedar box. Gently lifting the lid, she discovered a hand-carved gavel resting beside a polished round plate—the kind that echoed authoritative strikes in a courtroom.

A gasp of astonishment escaped her lips, and her eyes widened with appreciation. "Oh, Danny, this is amazing! A gavel and sound block? It's stunning," she exclaimed, running her fingers over the smooth woodwork.

Danny beamed with pride, his eyes reflecting a deep sense of satisfaction. "Knowing you, sis, I can't imagine you being content until you ascend to the bench as a judge someday. Hopefully, this will serve as a constant reminder and inspiration on your journey," he said, his voice filled with encouragement and belief in her potential.

Ginger turned her inquisitive gaze toward Danny. "How on earth did you manage to find the time to carve all of these incredible gifts?" she asked, a mix of admiration and curiosity in her eyes.

A mischievous grin played on Danny's face as he responded, "Well, after you left the workshop, something sparked my inspiration."

Shockwaves reverberated through the room, and a hushed silence settled in after Danny revealed the secret. The proverbial cat was out of the bag, and a collective gasp filled the air. He admitted that he and Ginger had ventured into the forbidden realm of Uncle Frank's workshop. The revelation hung in the air, creating a charged atmosphere of surprise and anticipation among those present.

"How could you, Danny?" his father's frustration and anger were palpable in his voice. The disappointment in his eyes reflected the breach of a well-established boundary. "Everyone knows that Uncle Frank explicitly requested that no one, absolutely no one, was to enter the workshop."

"Dad, Mom, please, just hear me out before passing judgment," Danny implored, sensing the weight of the transgression. "Yes, it's true, like a couple of wayward trespassers, we ventured into his workshop. For that, I sincerely apologize, but..." He paused, a hint of anticipation lingering in the air as he retrieved a binder from the garage. It had been discreetly planted under a couch pillow. Opening it, he carefully extracted a letter from Uncle Frank.

"Upon stepping into the forbidden workshop, we stumbled upon this binder," Danny began, his voice a mixture of apprehension and eagerness. "To my surprise, it held a letter specifically addressed to me from Uncle Frank." As he spoke, he delicately opened the letter, unfolding the mystery that had shrouded their actions.

The room fell into a weighted silence as Danny commenced reading the heartfelt words on the paper. A poignant atmosphere enveloped them, and tears welled up in the eyes of his mother and sister. In that moment, an unspoken understanding spread among them, including Danny's father – the realization that Uncle Frank had orchestrated this elaborate plan all along, leaving behind a carefully crafted legacy for each of them. The revelation added a profound layer of emotion to the air, turning a seemingly impulsive act into a poignant connection with the departed Uncle Frank.

A prolonged silence hung in the room, the weight of the revelation settling in. Eventually, it was Nancy who broke the quietude. "You know what? In my book, this ranks right up there as the best Christmas ever," she declared, her eyes still glistening from the emotional journey they had all experienced.

A chorus of agreements filled the room as small talk ensued, with everyone sharing their sentiments about the extraordinary turn of events. The atmosphere buzzed with a unique blend of joy and nostalgia, as they collectively marveled at how Uncle Frank, in his absence, had orchestrated a Christmas that transcended the ordinary. The room became a haven for shared memories and newfound appreciation for the bonds that extended beyond the tangible presence of a beloved family member.

Danny cleared his voice deliberately to get everyone's attention. "Well, sis, I agree with you that this is the best Christmas ever, but I needed to add something else to the mix." He looked at Ginger and held her hand. "Ginger and I are planning on getting married as soon as possible."

Cheers filled the room with Nancy and her mom rushing to Ginger to hug her and offer congratulations. Meanwhile, Danny's father rose and slowly walked over to his son. A beaming smile lit up his face as he extended a hand to Danny, giving him a firm handshake that conveyed a mix of pride and joy. "Danny, my boy, this is fantastic news! I couldn't be happier for both of you," he exclaimed, his eyes reflecting genuine happiness.

As the room buzzed with excitement and the anticipation of a wedding celebration, Danny's father continued, "You know, your Uncle Frank would have been over the moon about this. He always believed in the power of love and the importance of family." The mention of Uncle Frank brought a poignant moment of reflection to the gathering, a shared acknowledgment of the guiding presence he continued to exert over their lives.

"And, Danny," his father added, his voice softening, "remember how Uncle Frank saw the potential in your artistic talents? He knew that the workshop wasn't just a place for crafting wood but a sanctuary where your skills could shape something beautiful, something lasting. This engagement is another chapter in the legacy he envisioned for you."

In the ensuing months, Uncle Frank's vision unfurled like a well-crafted story. Danny and Ginger embarked on a new chapter of their lives, exchanging vows in an intimate ceremony held in a quaint church. Nancy stood by Ginger's side, radiantly serving as the maid of honor. As a delightful surprise, Nancy introduced her new boyfriend, a senior law student who shared her passion for Christmas. The family instantly embraced him, and his infectious love for the holiday season added an extra layer of warmth to their gatherings.

Uncle Frank's workshop, once a hidden gem, now buzzed with activity. Skilled craftsmen of all ages found solace and inspiration within its walls. The Santa letters contained in the room were slowly being addressed with toys being shipped as fast and Ginger could process them. Vendors orders were being answered with requests for more handcrafted toys.

A prominent sign proudly hung over the entrance, announcing the space as "Uncle Frank's Hidden Workshop." The legacy of Uncle Frank lived on, not just in the wooden creations but in the vibrant community of artisans he had inspired.

Upon entering the workshop, visitors were greeted by the majestic sight of Uncle Frank's wooden pirate ship proudly on display. Its intricate details captured the imagination of all who laid eyes on it, becoming a symbol of the artistry and craftsmanship that flourished within the workshop. The workshop had become a testament to Uncle Frank's foresight, a place where creativity flourished, and the love for woodworking was passed down through generations.

The air in the workshop resonated with the sounds of carving, the smell of wood chips, laughter, and the exchange of ideas, creating an atmosphere of camaraderie and shared passion. Uncle Frank's Hidden Workshop had transformed into a thriving hub, not just for wooden creations but for fostering a sense of community, echoing the spirit of Christmas throughout the year. As the wooden pirate ship continued to captivate visitors, it stood as a reminder of Uncle Frank's enduring legacy and the boundless possibilities that creativity and family could unlock.

Other books by the author:

JEANNIE LOOMIS THRILLER NOVELS:

Ark of the Covenant – Raid on the Church of Our Lady Mary of Zion

Star Chamber

Forgotten Plans

House of Special Purpose

Time Game

Thin Blue Line

The Fourth Reich

Black Heart/Black Cell

The Phantom Train

Rollercoaster

Snow Angel

The Fourth Reich Reborn

HORROR

House on Haunted Hill Resurrection

Beneath the Earth

The Tingler Unleashed

SEAL – Ghost Recon

Carnival of Lost Souls

www.ingramcontent.com/pod-product-compliance
Lightning Source LLC
Chambersburg PA
CBHW020548310726
48979CB00008B/1129/J

* 9 7 9 8 9 8 9 3 4 2 4 5 7 *